SON'S EYE

SON'S EYE

A Memoir

Charles E. Israel

Oakville, ON — Niagara Falls, NY

Canadian Cataloguing in Publication Data

Israel, E. Charles, 1920-1999
    Son's Eye: A Memoir

ISBN 0-88962-689-8

I. Israel, Charles E., 1920-1999   - Childhood and youth.
2. Authors, Canadian
(English)-20th century—Biography.* II. Title.

PS8517.S73Z53 1999   C813'.54   C99-932016-5
PR9199.3.I82Z53 1999

Published by MOSAIC PRESS, P.O. Box 1032, Oakville, Ontario, L6J 5E9, Canada. Offices and warehouse at 1252 Speers Road, Units #1&2, Oakville, Ontario, L6L 5N9, Canada and Mosaic Press, PMB 145, 4500 Witmer Industrial Estates, Niagara Falls, NY 14305-1386. Mosaic Press acknowledges the assistance of the Canada Council and the Dept. of Canadian Heritage, Government of Canada, for their support of our publishing programme.

Quotations from the songs *Blues in the Night and Till and Till We Meet Again* courtesy of Warner Bros. Publications

Copyright © 1999 Charles E. Israel
ISBN 0-88962-689-8
Printed and bound in Canada

THE CANADA COUNCIL | LE CONSEIL DES ARTS
FOR THE ARTS | DU CANADA
SINCE 1957 | DEPUIS 1957

Mosaic Press, Canada:
1252 Speers Road, Units #1&2,
Oakville, Ontario, L6L 5N9
Phone/Fax: 905-825-2130

Mosaic Press, In the USA:
PMB 145, 4500 Witmer Industrial Estates
Niagara Falls, NY 14305-1386
Phone/Fax:1-800-387-8992

email: cp507@freenet.toronto.on.ca

For Gloria

ONE

This is the way I always remembered it:

Early in the frigid December of 1932, several thousand desperate men and women from all over the United States converged on Washington, D.C. Some walked. A few drove decrepit cars or pickups. Most rode the rails, clinging to the tops of boxcars or huddled inside the empties.

Some were industrial workers who in the escalating hard times had lost lifelong jobs and were unable to find others. Some had owned farms, and when they could no longer muster cash for mortgage payments, the banks summarily threw them off the land. All of them arrived in Washington bereft and disoriented, but muzzily convinced that here at the heart of the government they had helped elect, they were bound to find redress.

They didn't expect to get their jobs or land back; they weren't that naive. But they couldn't believe that President Herbert Hoover and Congress were truly aware of the catastrophic turn their lives had taken. What they came to plead for now was food — not only for themselves and their families, but for all the many others across the nation who were slowly, hopelessly drifting toward starvation.

They knew the President had made a name for himself after the Great War providing sustenance to the famished millions of Europe. Once they had spoken their piece, made their plight known to him, surely

Mr. Hoover would find a way to ease their distress.

The Hunger Marchers, as the press instantly dubbed them, had no way of knowing that Mr. Hoover was as desperate as they. That he was sitting in the White House trembling, a lame-duck President watching the country unravel and wondering whether he could eke out the days till March, when he could sigh with relief and shove the whole stinking mess onto Franklin Roosevelt's plate. Hoover knew the unemployment figures. He was aware that venerable corporations and supposedly indestructible banks were toppling like dominoes. Nor was he a callous man. It pained him to realize that each passing day brought more supplicants to proliferating bread lines and soup kitchens. Most hurtful was the knowledge that an increasing number of the newly impoverished came from his beloved middle class, the phalanx of ardent supporters whom he had confidently promised a car in every garage, a chicken in every pot. Hoover knew well enough what was happening; he just hadn't a glimmer what to do about it.

So when he heard that hordes of shabbily dressed vagrants were advancing on the White House, he panicked. It never occurred to him to ask what the marching men and women might want. He simply concluded that they had to be the vanguard of some murderous Bolshevist rabble. The order went out from his office: Stop them.

An army detachment commanded by General Douglas MacArthur and his adjutant, a major named Dwight Eisenhower, ambushed the marchers about a mile from the White House and herded them onto a highway overpass spanning a desolate sweep of marshland. Soldiers with machine guns at either end of the bridge prevented the marchers from leaving. Escape over the sides of the bridge meant dropping more than a hundred feet onto the frozen marsh. No one tried. They languished on the bare concrete road for two days and nights without food, shelter or sanitary facilities and only minuscule rations of drinking water, while Mr. Hoover tried to make up his mind what to do about them.

My father, a rabbi in nearby Baltimore, was deeply troubled by what was happening in the nation's capitol. He was then 36, running a bit to fat as he had since boyhood, but tall and broad-shouldered, projecting an impression of burly power. He was no stranger to civil violence. A few years before, he had been a front-line observer of the workers' walkout against the Western Maryland Railroad, a notorious sweatshop organization. When management couldn't frighten the strikers off the picket line, it employed goons to bash in their heads. My father had denounced the company's brutality and injustice from his pulpit and in the press, and in the process attracted a number of extravagant physical threats. More recently, he had intervened on behalf of striking coal miners in Pennsylvania, again after having witnessed firsthand the oppressive conditions rampant in company towns.

On the third day of the Hunger Marchers' confinement, my father decided he had to do something. He took a train to Washington, bought as much food — bread, canned goods and the like — as he could cram into a taxicab. When the driver heard where he was supposed to go, he tried to dump both his fare and the cargo, but my father assured him he only wanted to deliver food to some hungry people, no one could possibly object to that, so really there wasn't the slightest chance of trouble.

It was a few minutes past five when they arrived at the western end of the bridge, but already it was dark, and bitterly cold. Two soldiers with rifles signaled the taxi to stop. My father got out, walked over to a sergeant warming his hands beside an oil-drum fire, identified himself and asked permission to take the load of food to the marchers. The sergeant looked my father over for a long moment while the wind whistled around them. "Get the fuck out of here," he said finally. My father responded politely that he would like to see the officer in charge. The sergeant stared at him, and my father realized courteous discourse was going nowhere.

He returned to the cab and eased in beside the driver. "Look," he said, "they don't want to let us go on." He peered through the windshield. Past the flimsy wooden barricade, shadowy figures were just visible in the feeble rays of the taxi headlights, hunched against the bridge railing, clustering in the lee shelter of a few wretched vehicles. "Those people haven't had a bite to eat for three days, I know I have no right to ask this. If you don't want to do it, okay, we'll just turn around and leave. But it would be easy to run your cab through that barricade."

The driver said nothing. My father glanced ahead once more, took a breath and went on. "I have to be fair and tell you they may shoot at us, but I don't really think they will. We'll probably get arrested, but by then the people in there will have a little food, and my guess is we'll get off with a fine. I'll see that yours is paid."

"This cab don't belong to me," the driver said, gazing uneasily past the barricade. "I'd get fired for sure. Listen, I got kids."

"Yes," my father said. "So have I."

Someone rapped on the driver's window. He rolled it down. The sergeant, stony-eyed. "Didn't I tell you to get the fuck out of here? Do it." And immediately, before the driver could reply, he kicked the door of the cab and bellowed,"Now!"

The driver rolled up the window, glanced at my father, put the taxi in gear and jammed the accelerator to the floor. The cab convulsed, then charged straight at the wooden barricade, maybe fifty yards away.

The machine gunners must have been waiting, fingers on triggers. They began firing at once. The cab veered crazily as all four tires were punctured, then lurched back on course and smashed through the barricade. The driver hit the brake, flung open his door and fled into the night, leaving the engine still idling.

My father lunged across from the passenger seat, grabbed the wheel and sent the taxi careering onto the bridge, its mercy cargo intact.

For most of my life I believed that story, exactly as I've set it down. I assumed I'd got the details directly from my father, and while he was alive it never occurred to me to question him further. Now and then over the many years since his death, doubts surfaced—anomalies of logic and character that I considered briefly and dismissed. I could have made an effort to verify the story; I knew the Baltimore and Washington papers would certainly have covered the Hunger Marchers. I never sought out a single file. As it turned out, I wouldn't have found much to help me, but that's not the point. I didn't even try.

* * *

The American Jewish Archives in Cincinnati has assembled a voluminous file on my father. Buried among the collected papers is his account of the night he spent with the Hunger Marchers, written for a journal called *The World Tomorrow* only a few hours after he returned to Baltimore.

There are numerous disparities between my memory of the incident and my father's account. Some are trivial, others far more significant. The three thousand men and women were penned up, not on a bridge but on an especially bleak segment of New York Avenue overlooking the Washington freightyards. The dropoff was almost perpendicular, more than a hundred feet down to a maze of track where rail traffic shunted ceaselessly. To the south an equally steep elevation rose from the edge of the road, and at intervals along the brow, men hunkered behind machine guns trained on the pathetic throng below.

Their captors were neither MacArthur nor Eisenhower, nor anyone in the military. It was the Washington police force that ambushed and imprisoned the marchers. On the evening of December 5, after they had been restrained under inhuman conditions for nearly 72 hours, my father was asked to speak for the American Civil Liberties Union at a Washington gathering protesting the illegal detention. At the last minute, the administrator of the Masonic Hall where the meeting was to be held summoned the organizers, returned their deposit and brusquely declared that the auditorium was no longer available. Neither, it appeared, was any other lecture or concert hall in the city. The organizers were forced to cancel the protest.

My father had not yet seen for himself what was taking place on New York Avenue. He made up his mind to do so now.

As he got out of the taxi that took him to the intersection of New York and Florida Avenues, he heard sirens. Several riot cars appeared out of the darkness and screamed past him, across the hastily lowered ropes of the police barrier. My father continued toward the pair of cops standing guard, trying to appear nonchalant but, as he expressed it, "with certain tremors of excitement and misgivings".

He fully expected to be turned away, but just at that moment a United Press reporter arrived and showed his ID. My father strode behind him, mumbling that he represented the ACLU, and the police waved them on. "I proceeded along about a quarter of a mile of vacant concrete highway," my father wrote. "I then came to the second group of policemen gathered by the hundreds. A little further on, behind a final barrier, were the Hunger Marchers. There were no excited speeches... The marchers were under perfect control of their leaders."

Many, however, were ill, victims of hypothermia and a lack of food and water. When my father arrived, the police Chief Inspector had apparently just realized that some of the marchers might die. Reluctantly, he gave permission for women and the most critically ill men to be transported out of the area in the marchers' vehicles.

There wasn't much rolling stock, and a number of sick marchers had to remain behind. The police crowded around those clambering into the rickety cars and pickups. They jostled, taunted and rapped them smartly with their clubs. "They've been doing that ever since we got here," a march leader said wearily to my father. "They're just aching for us to fight back. They can't wait to use their guns and gas bombs."

The miserable caravan crept away, inching between a double row of police who jeered and hammered on each car and truck as it passed. Then for a while there was silence except for the occasional shrill of a locomotive whistle and the shudder of clashing freight cars in the yard below.

My father stood in the darkness beside the march leader with whom he'd been talking. They were joined by a couple of Washingtonians, sympathizers with the marchers' cause who had, like my father, bluffed their way past the police sentries. Together they began to hatch a plan. Now that the police had allowed some of the marchers to leave, maybe they wouldn't detain the rest. Maybe all they had to do was walk past the barricade. Only they had to be careful. A mass exodus might give the police the excuse they'd been looking for to use gas and firearms.

Across the road, seven or eight reporters were pacing around a police car, stomping their feet on the concrete to keep warm, taking turns sitting in the car for a few moments of respite from the biting wind. Watching them, the march leader decided the plan was worth a try. At the very least, if they were turned back, the reporters would be witnesses that the Hunger Marchers were being forcibly detained.

They were turned back. The two dozen men only managed to venture a few steps beyond the barricade before their way was blocked by a cordon of police. An Inspector asked where they thought they were going. The leader calmly explained that housing had been provided in the city. He was taking the men to these homes. The Inspector didn't even hesitate. He raised his arm, and the police advanced, prodding the marchers backward with their clubs.

One of the cops grabbed my father and yelled, "Who the hell are you?" My father replied, trying to stay calm, "My name is Edward Israel. I'm a rabbi from Baltimore, and I'm here for the American Civil Liberties Union. I want to see if the civil rights of these men are being violated." The policeman laughed. "Are you kidding? These goddam bums got no rights."

But he took my father to the Chief Inspector. News of who my father was had apparently spread quickly. Several times as he and his escort walked past the clumps of police he heard the words, "Sheeny bastard."

The Chief Inspector, a man named Davis who questioned my father in a high, reedy voice, was no more cordial than his subordinates, but his PR sense appeared a tad more developed. My father never came right out and said that a group of Congressmen were on their way to New York Avenue, but he did imply he wouldn't be surprised if some turned up.

Davis grunted, turned his back on my father and walked away. An hour or so later, he told the march leaders that if they could prove they had accommodation for the marchers and were also able to supply transportation, they could start moving out.

In time a fleet of private cars and taxis began arriving. The barricade was torn down, the cars lined up, and the shivering marchers squeezed into them. The lead taxi began to roll.

From somewhere in the darkness machine gun fire stuttered. The tires on the first car went flat. And on the second. And the third and fourth, until seven vehicles sat crippled beside the wreckage of the barricade.

Chief Inspector Davis rushed forward, waving his arms and calling in his piping voice for the men to hold their fire. What he was looking at was the knot of reporters standing by, silently observing everything that went on.

The Chief Inspector needn't have been concerned. The *Washington Post* didn't mention the shooting episode or any of the indignities the marchers had endured, only referring to them as "pugnacious and rebellious". Another paper headed a story NO SIGNS OF HUNGER AMONG HUNGER MARCHERS, and none spoke of police brutality.

My father was furious with the press, publicly terming the coverage, or lack of it, "perverted journalism." But the main force of his rage was directed against President Hoover. My father had served on several of Hoover's hastily convened committees, frantic attempts to stave off housing and employment crises. In his opinion, these were token efforts; Hoover neither wanted to hear nor had any intention of following the Draconian advice his committee members offered.

The Hunger Marcher incident was final confirmation for my father that Hoover could scarcely find his way to the Presidential bathroom, let alone fashion deliverance for a country on the brink of ruin. However, that night he didn't—as a hero-worshipping son might have wished — storm over to the White House, batter down the door and, Isaiah-like, resoundingly denounce Hoover's cowardice and hypocrisy.

Instead he went home and caught a few hours of sleep. Then he sat down at his desk and wrote about what he had seen and what he thought it meant.

TWO

My father was born Edward Leopold Israel in Cincinnati, Ohio, on the next to last day of August, 1896. His father, Charles, had been born in Lithuania. While he was still a young boy, the family emigrated to Cincinnati. My grandfather remained there all his life and eventually become a successful insurance agent.

My mother's parents also lived in Cincinnati, so almost every summer during the 1920s my parents would load me, and later my younger brother, into a wheezy tan Peerless. We'd chug the 500 miles from Baltimore over the western Maryland mountains, through a drab tip of West Virginia and finally on to Ohio's Queen City. We'd stay about a month, and I loved every minute of it, mainly because of my Grandfather Israel.

I called him Paden — I have no idea why, but somehow even now it seems to suit his memory. He was an extraordinarily kind and lovable man. To me he came across as a series of appealing circles: his gently plump body; his spherical head almost completely bald, the gleam always discreetly talcumed; his little wire-rimmed glasses.

When I was about five, Paden began taking me to the movies two or three nights a week. The Forest Theatre was located in Avondale, then the center of Cincinnati's more upscale Jewish community. Lively food and clothing emporia mingled with squat brick apartment buildings along

Reading Road, and off this main thoroughfare radiated a network of sedate, opulent residential streets. Cincinnati is essentially a Southern city, and a summer day's heat could throb deep into the night. Paden and I would sit on backless wooden benches under the stars and watch Harold Lloyd, Tom Mix and even (viewing standards for kids then being somewhat laissez faire) Rudolph Valentino and Clara Bow. To help us appreciate what was happening on the giant screen, a diminutive woman with bleached hair robustly underlined on a piano every move of the mute images. If it rained—and it had to be a deluge, not just a passing summer shower—we moved next door, into a hot, musty hall where we'd sweat through the rest of the film while a relentless organ accompaniment made our eardrums tingle.

After the show, Paden and I would always go to a nearby soda fountain, where we'd select from a menu proclaiming literally hundreds of drinks: myriad enhancements of ice cream, fizzes, frappes, phosphates and a panoply of fruit mixtures. Paden and I would choose at random. Then we'd sit in our wire-backed chairs at our round marble table and talk about the funny things Harold Lloyd had done, or I'd ask him questions about what Valentino had been up to in that tent. I don't recall how Paden answered. A pity, because he was never patronizing (a gift he passed on to my father), so his replies must have been gems of diplomatic candor.

One night I found myself drinking the most delectable concoction I'd ever tasted. I had only pointed to a printed name when I'd ordered, and I was so ecstatic over what it was doing to my taste buds that I simply made loud noises with my straw instead of asking Paden what the drink was called. A few nights later, I hitched my chair close to the gleaming tabletop and asked eagerly for whatever it was I'd had last time. I can still see Paden's consternation and recall my own when we both realized he didn't know. But he put his hand over mine and quietly asked me to tell him how it tasted. I tried. We held an earnest conference with a freckled soda jerk and ordered what he advised, prompted by my recollection. No luck.

Nor did we get it right the next time. Or the next. Night after night we'd order pairs of unknown drinks, seeking the ambrosia. Some were delicious, but still there was a sense of disappointment. Paden never seemed to consider the quest trivial, and he never lost patience. And alas, we never found what we were looking for. Decades later, I began to taste and write about wines professionally. Sometimes when I'd be tracking down an especially subtle, puzzling flavor, I'd think about that soda fountain. About the ceiling fans rotating languidly, stirring warm air redolent of vanilla and something citrusy and the mellow-acrid marriage of chocolate and carbonated water. About the sweetness and elusiveness of sensory memory. And about the middle-aged man in a striped shirt with a stiff white detachable collar and the small boy, bare legs dangling over the edge of his chair. Their heads close together, murmuring.

I believe my grandfather knew almost everyone in Cincinnati, and everyone he knew adored him. But when they inevitably said of him, "Charlie Israel is a saint," I suspect the main reason was because for half a century he suffered the presence of my grandmother without (so far as anyone knew) a whisper of complaint.

Searching for Emma Linz Israel's redeeming qualities is not a rewarding task. As a young woman she must have been exceptionally beautiful. I remember her only from middle age on. By then her figure had grown lumpy, and her face possessed an odd, almost luminescent, pallor. What I recall most clearly, though, were her eyes. They were extremely wide-set, heavy-lidded and filled with a somber, fermenting power. But photos taken in her early twenties show her limpid-eyed, with a delicate complexion, pert, engaging features and luxuriant dark hair intricately tiered in a *fin de siecle* coiffure. True, in every likeness a slightly combative set of the jaw is discernible. But smitten young men seldom make analytical studies of their fiancees' jawbones, and in any event, Emma very likely reined in her aggressions during courtship.

God knows she didn't after they were married. Her tongue was restless and barbed, and apparently she rarely turned it off. According to family legend, she would warm up on my father and his younger brother whenever she caught sight of them during the day. Then late in the afternoon when my grandfather would return home, Emma would begin her main-event harangue. She was inventive, able to embroider her text vividly through the evening, and by the small hours she would often just be hitting the peroration. Her message was consistent: my grandfather was a failure, a laughable excuse for a man, and she'd been an idiot to marry him when she'd had so many opportunities to do so much better.

When I got old enough to be aware of what was going on, I was chronically furious on my grandfather's behalf. And amazed that he neither retaliated nor even seemed to want to. Years later, after a number of troubled relationships and a pair of failed marriages, I'm finally beginning to understand both the beauty and the peril of mutual need. And the convoluted, wordless contracts we make with each other to perpetuate that need.

Who after all can chart the anatomy of my grandmother's demons? At the time, probably, least of all she. Maybe my grandfather himself set her wild: her sense of the power that lay behind his gentleness—a subterranean strength that might have matched hers—and her resentment because he chose not to deploy it.

Not long after they married, Emma fell into ill health. Or thought she did. Every local doctor she visited told her there was nothing wrong, but she dismissed their assurances and sought out specialists in distant cities. Ultimately she discovered her own symbiotic soulmate back home in Cincinnati, a surgeon whose skill with the knife was exceeded only by his eagerness to use it.

Each operation—and there were without exaggeration dozens, many of them major—exuded theatrical flair. Early on, the entire family was genuinely concerned, standing vigil at the hospital, hanging on the surgeon's breathless bulletins. Emma was very brave, Emma was fighting for her life, Emma had suffered a relapse but was beginning to improve. Then the day following one abdominal exploratory, someone surprised her deliberately tearing open her stitches. After this, her audiences dropped away, until even my father and his brother could no longer muster enough filial commitment to make the journey from the cities where they lived.

Finally there was nothing left to cut. And by the end of her life she had become a junkie, addicted to the morphine the surgeon so bounteously dispensed during their long professional tour together. Fortunately, by then my grandfather had died. Had he been alive, doubtless he would have been out on a perpetual prowl, scouring the Cincinnati riverfront, or across the bridge in Kentucky, ransacking the lower depths of Covington in search of his wife's next fix. And if she had died before him, he would have mourned her profoundly.

Two qualities Emma possessed in abundance were vitality—without which she could never have survived her incredible spate of surgical adventures—and single-mindedness. She passed these qualities on, happily in a less crazed form, to her younger son Dorman, a pioneer in radio engineering who went on to a distinguished career in research and manufacturing.

The manic edge of Emma's single-mindedness cut a bit of a swathe through my father. Paden's genes protected him to some extent. But he did do what he wanted when he wanted to do it, and this willfulness helped kill him. In his mid-teens he contracted rheumatic fever and refused to endure the prescribed lengthy convalescence. He loved football, his bulk made him a formidable guard, and he wasn't about to pass up a season. The resulting strain marked the start of what was to become severe cardiac deterioration.

Early on he decided to become a rabbi. My grandfather came from a traditional background — not inflexibly Orthodox but conservative enough to observe the dietary laws. Before marriage, my grandmother promised to maintain a kosher house. She did, for about two weeks. Then one day, without warning, she opened the pair of cupboards containing the rigidly sequestered meat and dairy dishes, hurled a sizable number of each out a window, and shuffled the remnants together into a single cupboard. She then announced, perhaps a bit redundantly at that point, "Your religion's nothing but dishes and pots and pans, and I'm through with it!"

Paden, characteristically, uttered no protest. Had he chosen to do so, many things might have turned out differently. My father, for example, might have attended a conservative rabbinical seminary, quite possibly altering the entire dynamic of his ministry.

There were, however, other influences at work besides Emma's noisy nailing of her proclamation to the kitchen door. Cincinnati was the New World heart of Reform Judaism, a vigorous movement that had begun about a century before in Germany. Reform leaders believed the Jewish faith should be understandable to its followers, rather than ritual by rote. They also felt that in a modern world some of the more stringent precepts — such as not riding in a vehicle on the Sabbath — had become outmoded. Most Orthodox rabbis regarded Reform's departures as heretical. But to many American Jews, just because it was accessible, explanatory rather than peremptory, Reform became increasingly attractive.

The Hebrew Union College, which trained rabbis for Reform congregations, was located in Cincinnati. Theoretically, students were supposed to have a B.A. degree before entering. In fact, most completed their undergraduate work mornings at the University of Cincinnati, and in the afternoon took graduate courses at HUC.

My father was ordained in 1919, in absentia because halfway through his senior year he volunteered to go overseas as a chaplain. He served six months in France, a considerable amount of which was spent writing fevered letters to the woman who was to become his wife. He had met her only weeks before leaving for Europe, but apparently decided at once that they were going to marry. My mother made a few perfunctory cautious noises, but she never had a chance. Emma's elemental wildness whistled through the pages of my father's letters like artillery shells. All that ardor must have overwhelmed my mother, and maybe also frightened her a little. Not so much the words themselves, but their intensity, their unpredictability. Their compellingness.

They married, spent a few years with small congregations in Springfield, Illinois and Evansville, Indiana, where I was born. Late in 1923, my father took over the pulpit of the Har Sinai Temple in Baltimore.

The affairs of this affluent congregation were mainly conducted by a handful of German-Jewish mercantile families whose forebears had established themselves in Baltimore early in the 19th century. Politically, most of Har Sinai's officers occupied territory between hidebound and die-hard. When they hired him, my father was 27, young to be the spiritual leader of such influential citizens. Surely during their several interviews they must have picked up an inkling of his political persuasions, even if he made an effort to keep them under wraps. They also would have made their own beliefs unmistakably clear to my father. Yet one of his early sermons was entitled "Rugged Individualism — Is It Our Answer?" For him, the question was rhetorical, and he told the rugged individualists sitting before him why.

Over the next few years he also told them why they should espouse birth control, a minimum wage, public housing and unemployment insurance. The Temple's board of directors rumbled a little, but surprisingly didn't interfere. Some of their apparent tolerance may have been because my father was rapidly acquiring a national reputation, and the congregation relished the reflected glory. He sat on a spectrum of municipal, state and federal committees dealing with social issues. Nor were all his concerns secular. In 1930, on the stage of Baltimore's fusty old Lyric Theater, he debated the merits of religion with Clarence Darrow, and appears to have better than held his own against the wily old disbeliever. He was a good pastor. He and my mother visited ailing congregants regularly. He was also known as an able counselor who dispensed compassionate but practical advice.

He ran into trouble, though, with one of his most fervent causes, prison reform. He was convinced that the governor and his appointees were covering up corruption and brutality at the Maryland State Penitentiary. He accused them, publicly and often. The governor, a white-haired patrician, lashed back, advising my father's employers not to allow him on the streets without a muzzle. Suddenly it wasn't glory that was reflecting on the congregation and especially its officers. They let my father know they were not amused. He replied from the pulpit. "You may sincerely feel that because of my official position, I have no right to interest myself in public controversies where I feel a moral issue is at stake. If this is your point of view, I am sorry that I cannot follow you in it. As I interpret religion, it is the application of the individual conscience to the problems of life... For one to keep silent merely because he may be expressing an adverse opinion is a type of moral cowardice to which I cannot submit... As far as the present instance is concerned, I have been trying for some months to secure an open and untarnished examination of our penal system. I have been motivated in this by a sincere feeling that our present system is a social menace."

When you look at them on a printed page, many of my father's sermons come off as slightly awkward. But there's never any doubt about what he meant to say, and in this case he was laying his job on the line. (The board, incidentally, backed down. My father kept pounding away at the governor, and eventually got his impartial investigation and an appreciable alleviation of conditions in the Pen.) What my father's printed words almost never convey is his oratorical genius. When he stepped up to the pulpit or rose to address a rally, an odd transformation took place. Suddenly Paden and Emma were combined, annealed in an eerie white heat. Warmth and wrath, easy geniality with a dangerous edge. It was always impossible to predict what my father would say first, or next, or how. Even his fiercest critics conceded that he was brilliant.

He was also arguably one of the biggest damn fools I've ever known.

He drove his personal life out onto a tightrope and kept it teetering there till the day he died. He wounded my mother grievously; the scars endured all her life. Nor does it excuse him to say that his suffering often matched and sometimes exceeded hers. He tested the affection and fanatic loyalty of his many friends well past any conventional breaking point. He stunted my brother emotionally and along the way took a few pretty good gouges out of me. I was aware while he was alive that he had feet of clay. It's taken me almost until now to learn how far up toward his hips the clay really extended. I loved him very much. I still do.

The memories leapfrog and tumble. Back of the house where we lived the longest, past my mother's roses and peonies and a low bushy hedge, mint grew wild. I'd nip off a few fragrant sprigs with my thumbnail and carry them to the kitchen. My father would crush leaves in a syrup of bourbon and sugar while I used a wooden mallet to pulverize ice cubes wrapped in an old dishtowel. Meanwhile Sedonia, the black, Baptist, teetotal, affectionately devoted woman who cooked for us would cluck, mutter and clatter pots. My father and I drank our juleps sitting on the back porch. Sometimes we'd talk, sometimes not. We could see Tyson's Riding Academy, an ancient frame house and long, low stables, across an expanse of open field. It was usually late afternoon, and often the setting sun would tint the returning riders red-gold.

He used to take me to baseball games, in the Orioles' old park, long before they moved up to the majors. We'd sit in the heat along the first-base line and bound up and yell whenever an Oriole belted a solid hit, while we made sticky messes of our fingers and mouths with Eskimo Pies. Long before I could read, my father was showing me how to inscribe the proper symbols on the scorecard for walk, strikeout and hit.

He had been a zealous pacifist all his life. Relinquishing this conviction was excrutiating for him, but by the spring of 1940, he became glumly certain that only force could stop the Nazis. I was then studying for the rabbinate, completing my first year at HUC. My political stance had moved left of my father's, and I was vehemently opposed to any American involvement in Europe. He was tolerant, even to the extent of allowing me to preach an anti-war sermon from his pulpit when I returned to Baltimore in June.

But the next month, at the cottage the family rented on a Maine lake, we argued more or less constantly. To his credit, he never once reminded me that I was 19 years old. Our disagreement, though, grew sharper. One night we ended up screaming at each other and went to bed not speaking. Before the fracas, we had made plans to go fishing at dawn. I stood beside the shore, still pretty mad, watching grey light filter through the pines and wondering if he'd show. He did, silently. I shoved the boat away from the dock, yanked on the starter cord of the outboard, and we putt-putted downlake toward a spot we had agreed the day before might be promising for bass.

The sun was starting to curl around the mist as I cut the engine and used the oars to pull us through a weed-choked narrows. Neither of us had yet spoken a word. I dropped the anchor in deep water off a ridge of rock. We cast. The ripples died. We continued to sit without looking at each other. Then suddenly we both turned at once, I making a pacifying gesture, he a grimace. We laughed and hugged each other's shoulders. Then we settled back to fish.

When I was about eight, I began going with my parents to the Temple for Saturday morning services. My father wore a black morning coat and striped trousers. No prayer shawl and no head covering; Har Sinai was staunchly Reform. Much earlier its rabbis had sported something called a pulpit hat, a black tricorn that seemed to cry out for jester's bells. Wisely, the congregation had voted to abolish it but had refused to legislate yarmulkes for the sanctuary.

After services I would usually go with my parents to a delicatessen near the Temple. The waitresses were all middle-aged and ample-bosomed. This was borderline South, so they moved a little lethargically, and their Yiddish-inflected speech contained just a hint of drawl. But their message was identical to the one you'd hear a few hundred miles north on Sixth Avenue: Listen, the chicken's very special, you won't be sorry, listen I'm telling you take the chicken. I always had the same lunch—sardine sandwich with a slice of raw onion, a scoop of potato salad, a sour pickle and a bottle of lurid-colored grape soda. I realize now that on many Saturdays, as I sat there avidly wolfing down that gourmet combination, I was probably the only reason my parents were making an effort to speak to each other. Some Saturdays—I guess when the atmosphere became too tense for even my presence to mitigate—we'd skip the deli and drive straight home. My mother would hurry upstairs, while my father and I would go out to the kitchen and open cans of Stegners' mock turtle soup and chili, which we'd top off with pickles so sour they brought tears to our eyes.

Even when I was very young he talked to me. Mainly when we were driving somewhere. No doubt he talked to me in the summer, but what I seem to recall most clearly are the winter soliloquies. He wore an old grey tweed overcoat that bunched up around his shoulders. He treated the road like an adversary and the car as a weapon, but I was seldom afraid. His voice was always calm and gentle, wistful I realize now. I only remember fragments of what he talked about, but piecing some of the shards together many years afterward, I'm aware they made up an appalling burden for a father to unload onto a small son. But also, I guess today, there must have been a loneliness so monumental, so raw that it had to be articulated. Even after hearing from therapists later in life how damaging this might have been, I've never begrudged my father these moments.

As I plunged into adolescence, the pendulum swung the other way and I mainly did the talking. Also mainly in the car. I knew he was preoccupied with many other things, but every time I talked to him, I was sure he was listening. However, he never offered advice. Not until—which I didn't do every time—I turned to him and asked: What do you think?

My father had a bad heart attack in 1930 and another about three years later. He was then working at least twelve hours every day of the week. Smoking a couple of packs of cigarettes a day didn't improve his condition. More and more he suffered from severe angina.

He had begun his ministry opposed to Zionism. The Third Reich helped turn him around, and in addition to his congregational duties and a dozen social action committees, he began speaking at rallies all over the country in support of the Jewish homeland.

In the spring of 1939 I made up my mind to become a rabbi. I applied to the Hebrew Union College and was admitted for the fall term, providing I passed the entrance exam. I had learned just enough Hebrew to treble my way through my bar mitzvah portion, then backed away from further study. My father had never pushed me to continue. Now, however, I was saying I had a goal. He believed that if you wanted something, you went after it. He would help me learn enough Hebrew to pass the exam. I dropped out of the spring term at the University of North Carolina. The day I arrived home, my father presented me with a Hebrew Bible and a pristine copy of Davidson's Grammar. We set up a schedule.

We both should have known better. He had taught me to drive. His chief pedagogical method was to light his very short fuse the instant he settled himself in the passenger seat. It invariably exploded soon after I pulled away from the curb, somewhere between second and third gear.

The Hebrew course was fairly pure disaster right from the start. We would sit on either side of a table, blinking at each other through cigarette smoke. I was matching his daily two packs by now, though as an expression of independence I had chosen Camels in preference to his green-wrapped Lucky Strikes. Sometimes, though, we'd make a tacit compromise and split a deck of Chesterfields. "Hebrew is a beautiful language," he'd say to me. "But if you're just going to vegetate there and refuse to learn the fundamentals, how do you ever expect to master the nuances?" Or, more to the point, "Come on, come *on*! You were supposed to *memorize* those inflections! How can anybody so bright be so lazy? Well, maybe I've been overestimating your intelligence. If you're not up to it, I suppose we could take it a little slower. But goddamit, son, there's no time!" This could make me pretty nervous.

One afternoon while I was lighting a Camel, forgetting I already had two glowing away in the ashtray, I saw my father's face go pale. He clenched his fist and pressed it against his chest. In no time perspiration was beading his forehead. I had seen him in pain before, but never like this. I asked if I should phone the doctor. He shook his head and reached in his pocket for the vial of nitroglycerine tablets. "It'll pass," he said.

But it didn't. He groaned, then cried out. I knew my father hated giving in to pain, but this was ridiculous. I started to get up. "No," he whispered. "No!" I sat down again and involuntarily reached across the table. He grabbed my hand and held onto it. I squeezed back, as hard as I could.

I don't know how long we sat like that, staring into each other's eyes. Finally he began to relax, and to breathe deeply. We eased our desperate grip. He gave my hand a last little pressure, released it and sat up very straight. "Well!" he barked. "What are you waiting for?" But the next day we agreed it would be better if I continued my preparation with one of his colleagues.

By the mid-thirties he had added chairing the mayor's committee on employment stabilization and arbitrating Baltimore's clothing industry disputes to his schedule. He attracted Roosevelt's attention and began serving on various Presidential commissions. Almost every month he would be summoned to testify at Senate hearings on social legislation.

In the spring of 1941 the Union of American Hebrew Congregations, which represented nearly all Reform Jewry in the United States, asked him to become its executive director. The Union was then headquartered in Cincinnati. My father felt the organization was stagnating in Ohio. He wanted to move it to Washington. Many on his executive board opposed the move. They feared my father was trying to politicize the Union. He knew a spate of arm-twisting lay ahead, in connection with the move and some other galvanizing measures he had in mind. The challenge excited him.

That fall I began my third year at HUC. I lived in the dorm, and when my father came to Cincinnati for his installation as head of the Union, he asked to stay in a dormitory suite rather than a downtown hotel. Partly this was so he and I could have more time together. But he also liked being with young people. HUC students, however, have never acted like ordinary young people. We knew we had been selected to be leaders and we never let ourselves forget it. We were intelligent, articulate, urbane, wearily cynical and almost totally insufferable.

Yet when my father walked into a roomful of students, it was meltdown time. He could banter with them, match their terrible jokes. When they spoke seriously, he listened seriously, and when he replied, it was always in a quiet, casual tone. One night I came into the "Bumming Room", which was what we called our lounge on the ground floor. A dozen students stood in a rapt circle around my father, listening. "Ring around the roly," I said into the silence when he finished, not without a twinge of jealousy.

On Sunday morning, October 19, I was walking out of the dormitory on my way to teach a class at an Avondale synagogue. The dining room window flew open and my father, who had just come downstairs for breakfast, leaned out. "Don't forget dinner," he called. "See you this evening."

My girlfriend Lee and I were supposed to meet him at six in the lobby of the Netherland Plaza Hotel. At three twenty-four, in the middle of a speech to his executive board, he pitched forward onto the table and died instantly.

He was 45 years old.

THREE

I'm sitting in my apartment in Toronto, the city Peter Ustinov so tellingly characterized a while ago as New York run by the Swiss. Okay, New York is more exciting, but a dollop of Swiss stodge can be comforting. I find as I get older, though I still enjoy forays into the nervier venues, I no longer get the rush I once did from the presence of incipient violence.

Anyhow, there are enough reminders of that even in Toronto. Our apartment lies close to the city core. The room where I'm writing overlooks a lush ravine, and beyond it a six-lane viaduct. The bridge traverses a major parkway and also acts as a conduit for ambulances en route to several nearby hospitals. I hear the sirens and hooters every fifteen minutes or so. Some of the ambulance passengers are victims of traffic accidents, others of domestic savagery. Probably a number have been felled by cardiac arrest. I guess at the moment when I hear an ambulance shriek by on the viaduct, I think heart attack because of what I've just written about my father.

But always the ambulance signifies an abrupt cessation. One minute you're proceeding with your life— happily, unhappily, whatever. The next you're no longer in control. You may die, you may already be dead.

As I got closer to the age of 45, I found myself becoming even more tense and irascible than usual. It took me a while to realize what was

21

upsetting me. I was in perfect health, but my father had died at 45, and I had no right to expect to live longer than he had. Forty-five was a kind of sound barrier, and like the early jet planes, as I approached it I was buffeting. I've been told since that what I experienced is a common phenomenon. I may have even sensed it at the time. That didn't prevent the absurd sense of relief I felt the morning of my forty-sixth birthday. Nor the very slight pang of guilt.

Now I'm well into my seventies, and again I find myself contemplating death. Not too often, and not at all morbidly, but with a growing sense of intimacy. To use the apt British expression, I'm still in rude health, I enjoy almost everything I do, and I want to live much longer. But if I can't, I want to go swiftly. As my father did. What I dread most, what I believe all of us fear after we exceed the biblical threescore and ten, is slow deterioration, the descent to helplessness, the interminable terminal illness and a dependency on machines and palliative drugs. Should that happen to me, I hope I still have the power to end it quickly. Or that my wife does, and will. Or my doctor.

Euthanasia. At the time my father died, it was only beginning to be a politico-ethical question. Much of the discussion then was clouded by what we were just learning about the intentions of the Nazis. So many issues since then. How would my father feel about genetic engineering, the disintegration of the Soviet Union, the bigotry and cruelty practiced by some Israelis in the name of God and the Holocaust? Ridiculous speculation. What will I say from the grave about the contentious issues of 2041?

I'm aware as I muse away here that what I'm really doing is temporizing. The doubts again. Not the sharp uneasiness I once felt, but nagging, still there.

When I first got the idea I wanted to write something about my father, I didn't anticipate any real problems. I've been a fulltime writer for more than 40 years. I've done books, articles, movies, radio and television plays. Some of what I've written has been autobiographical, so I was sure I'd be able to handle most of the tricky personal aspects. But when I started work on this project I thought I knew the worst there was to know about my father. One thing that happened was I discovered I didn't.

I have an aunt—my uncle Dorman's widow—who lives in White Plains, New York. Fran is in her nineties, bright and articulate, very lively; one of her few laments is that her golf partners keep dying off. She dropped out of a promising university career, as women were expected to do when they got married in the early 1920s, but all her life she's done extensive volunteer work for the blind and at a cancer research institute. She's a little imperious and quite outspoken, in the manner of the title personality of *Driving Miss Daisy*. I enjoy her company, and she likes recalling anecdotes from when she and Dorman and my parents were young. Soon after I began my research, I visited her in White Plains and told her I was planning to write a memoir about my father. She was delighted.

Fran and I talk straight to each other, and I mentioned that one element I knew I was going to have trouble with was my father's lover. Fran was shaken. She obviously hadn't known anything about Selma, and this shook me. But I'd begun, so I had to go on. Selma and her husband had been members of my father's congregation. As far as I knew, the affair continued for some years, and at the time of his death, my father intended to divorce my mother and marry Selma.

Fran listened without saying much. I knew I had distressed her, and I was sorry. But she seemed to roll with it, and we didn't discuss the subject again for the rest of my visit, nor in phone conversations over the next while. Then, just before starting to write, I made a final research swing to New Haven, Baltimore and Washington, searching for some last vital pieces of information. I stayed overnight in White Plains. It didn't take Fran long to bring up what was on her mind. "Are you still going to write about that business of your father having an affair?" And before I could say anything, "I think it's a big mistake, and I'm very concerned."

In the car on the way to her country club for dinner I tried to explain that Selma was a meaningful part of my father's life. And since I wasn't attempting a eulogy, I had to include whatever I knew, the good and the not so good. What I didn't tell Fran was that since our last meeting I had turned up a few other odds and ends, and I *was* having problems with these.

We arrived at the club just as I finished my rationale. She was winding up to respond, but the dining room was full and more boisterous than usual. Both Fran and I have hearing problems, and crowds often render us uncomprehending. She turned her aid down, I took mine out. We're both accomplished trencherpersons, and we paid close, silent attention to scallop and shrimp hors d'oeuvre and thick, rare lambchops. I did expect, though, that she'd be on my case as soon as we got back in the car. She spoke not a word all the way to her apartment. Only when we had settled into leather armchairs in the library did she say quietly, "What really concerns me is this. Your father was a brilliant man who did a lot of wonderful things in his time. If he had lived, he would have accomplished much more, and he probably would have become famous enough to be remembered even today. But he died young. Today very few people have even heard of him. You're going to revive the memory of your father, but I'm afraid what you're planning to do will diminish the man and his name. Why bring him back to life at all if what you're going to do is make him seem less than he was?"

Fran knew the right buttons to push. I was already thinking about fudging the biographical material I'd been accumulating by converting it into a novel. It would give me narrative freedom, and nobody else would get crowded. But each time I got close to deciding fiction was the answer, something made me shy away. More and more strongly I felt I had to try and tell it as it actually happened, or not tell it at all. I seriously considered the latter.

But what I kept coming back to was the two versions of the Hunger Marcher story. The way I had beefed up and sloughed off elements of the actual incident to create the image I seemed to need. My father the invincible white knight. I wove the fantasy in my early teens, and I kept it wrapped around me until I was nudging old age.

At any point from my late twenties on I could have come to terms with the truth. Having survived a couple of years of the War by then, I could have better understood my father's feelings that December night in 1932. The cold, the darkness, the uniforms. His frail health, angina probably tightening its iron band around his chest as he walked behind the United Press man, past the police sentries. Popping nitroglycerine pills as he crossed the windswept stretch of concrete. The hostility and viciousness of the police, the clubs and the guns, the uncertainty over if, when and how they would use them. My father almost surely terrified, but standing up to each confrontation.

And instead of driving a taxi filled with food through a fusillade of machine gun bullets, he wrote this: "The colossal stupidity of the whole proceedings was its worst aspect. Here came a group of men and women into the heart of our government asking the constitutional right of petition and protest, and promising to leave within a few days. No crowd has ever functioned more obediently under a more responsible leadership. If they had been allowed to present their petition and make their protest and depart, the whole matter would have passed over quietly. Instead, they were imbued with a conviction that, at the very center of American democracy, the underdog has no chance. It is such tactics which are gnawing at the roots of the sound structure of American life. The Washington police in their treatment of the Hunger Marchers did more violence to American institutions than could ever have been accomplished by permitting these ragged victims of unemployment to stand on their soap boxes and harangue their audiences with the most revolutionary doctrines."

Once I discovered what he had really done that night, and accepted it, I had at least an intimation of the story I wanted to try and tell. But that was later. When I began my research, I had the flawed man whose frailties I incompletely understood. I had the friend who was also my father. And I had the hero I had compelled myself to construct.

I wasn't sure what to do with any of them.

FOUR

The rain that had been threatening all morning finally came down in sheets just north of Dayton, reducing visibility on the I-75 almost to zero. I eased the Toyota over into the slow lane and kept on singing. Ever since I left the motel I'd been rummaging memory for songs popular during my years at HUC. I was amazed at how many of the words came back, less surprised at how my voice cracked and quavered anywhere near a high note. This didn't matter the way it once might have. At midyear break during my second year at HUC, I returned to Baltimore with a fierce cold, coughing incessantly. "Stop that," my father ordered. "Do you want to wreck your voice?" Unreasonable, and we both knew it. But we were also like divas, he and I, cosseting the instrument, so I turned my face crimson repressing the cough.

I was pleased to find associations—of whatever sort—starting to surface more freely. After a few months of preparatory letters, I was just jumping into the actual research, and feeling a little iffy. I intended to mine the Archives in Cincinnati, but I had no idea what I'd find. I was also trying not to pin too many hopes on Dr. Marcus.

Jacob Rader Marcus was 94 and the only living contemporary of my father I knew of. They'd been HUC classmates. After ordination, Marcus obtained a doctorate in Berlin, then returned to join the HUC faculty, and to begin turning out books on his specialty, American Jewish history. I recalled him from the days when he'd taught me, a rangy, slightly stooped man with a great beak of a nose and restless eyes, striding the classroom aisles as he lectured. His memory was prodigious. Mention a town on the Louisiana bayou or a Badlands hamlet in South Dakota, and without hesitation he would name the first Jewish settler and continue with a flood of rich anecdotes about the community's social history. I'd heard he was getting frail, but not only was he playing with a full deck, he could still shuffle several at once. He supervised the Archives, taught a day every week at the College, and kept two shifts of secretaries and researchers busy from morning till midnight.

I'd also been warned that he could be abrupt and bristly. Not for him, apparently, to go gentle into some good Mr. Chips night. There was, however, no hint of this in the letter he'd written me. "May I say, and I am speaking objectively, your father was a very distinguished person. His early death was a calamity for this country. I will be only too happy to see you if you come to Cincinnati and want to talk about your father. I knew a great deal about him, at least I think I did. Inasmuch as I am psychiatrically oriented, I will give you an honest evaluation, warts and all."

I'd smiled over the "psychiatrically oriented" and looked forward to our meeting. I hadn't seen or even kept in touch with Dr. Marcus since I dropped out of the College in 1943. But then over the years I'd very carefully avoided contact with almost everyone connected with HUC. Or Jewish religious life, for that matter.

The rain was letting up a bit. I maneuvered the Toyota cautiously around a creeping semi. *My mama done told me*, I sang to the clack of the wipers, *when I was in kneepants...*

My girlfriend Lee and I bellowing the words on a Friday evening, driving the 30 miles from Cincinnati to Lawrenceburg, Indiana. My bi-weekly, as the periodic visits were called. Towns with too small a population to support a fulltime rabbi made arrangements for an HUC student to conduct services every other week.

Ten miles from Lawrenceburg we'd start to detect the nutty-pungent odor of mash, which would become overpowering by the time we drove through the entrance gate of the distillery that controlled the town. My synagogue was a lounge adjacent to the building where they did the distilling, round the clock now that the U.S. was in the War. I never knew when my earnest recitation of the liturgy would be punctuated by a hoarse release of pent-up steam.

When I first went to Lawrenceburg, I preached sermons no one understood. They sat there in front of me, that lot of poor tired chemists and shopkeepers, politely allowing me to ramble through flights of Judaeo-Marxist lyricism. But after the third or fourth sermon even they rebelled. They complained to Lee, and she gentled the message for me. I was with them a year and a half after that, so either I did better or they simply learned how to close their eyes and think of Zion.

Driving back to Cincy, harvest moon riding the Ohio Valley. Lee snuggled close, blonde head on my shoulder, her voice a sleepy whisper:

"A man is a two-face, A worrisome thing Who'll leave you to sing The blues in the night."

The rain had stopped, but the clouds still lowered, clusters of lumpy grey balloons in the November sky. I could feel myself starting to get uncomfortable. I was going to stay in the dormitory. I'd be there soon. I hadn't set eyes on the College for 47 years. Nor had I even wanted to.

My father guessed, and brought the subject up while we were fishing in the rain. We did a lot of that, those summers in Maine. For one thing, we were both addicts and hated to miss even a day of trying to hook that venerable, evasive bass that lurks at the bottom of every wilderness lake. We hated raingear because it was cumbersome and hot, so we got drenched and warded off chill by passing a bottle of Scotch back and forth.

"You're restless," my father said. I think I tried a flippant reply, jiggled the bait can, reeled in some line, things like that. I had just finished my second year at the College, and he was right and I wasn't sure why. He waited, rainwater dripping off his chin and the end of his nose. We passed the bottle. Finally I nodded. My father let out his breath.

"We'll talk about why in a while. If you want. I suspect you may not know why, and I may be able to guess, but I could be very wrong. I understand the feeling, though, and I just want to say this." He stopped and turned a little away. I watched the rain zigzag shreds of light across the black surface of the lake. "I think you know how happy I was when you said you wanted to become a rabbi," he said after a moment. "But I'd be devastated if you stopped wanting to and only went on with it to please me." He turned to me now. "I mean that, son."

Two months later he was dead.

We never did talk about my reasons for being restless. Mainly it was because I really couldn't express them, and my father didn't crowd me. Over the next couple of years I was able to get the reasons up where I could see and think about them. Skepticism about theology and prayer. Anger against the hypocrisy of organized religion, the pettiness of congregants I would be expected to deal with, their eagerness, compulsion even, to turn a rabbi into a dancing bear. All those sharp young edges. Problems that now, after the passage of years, I'd probably be able to deal with. Isn't that what maturity is supposed to be: the strength to fight for what you can change, the wisdom to accept what you can't? Today I might be able to accommodate what I couldn't in 1943.

I hope I'd be sorry if I tried and succeeded.

* * *

I parked at the foot of the driveway and sat looking up at the College. As a campus it had always seemed more homely than inspiring—a ragtag of stocky buildings perched above staid Clifton Avenue, fronted by a comfortable sweep of lawn. How could such an unprepossessing collection of weathered brown brick generate and sustain 47 years of anxiety dreams?

Actually, there were only two or three a year, but invariably I woke up from them sweating. Always they had to do with my poverty of knowledge. Usually I'd be returning to HUC classes after years of absence, but the interchangeable professor would act as if I'd never left. He'd bombard me with questions I couldn't answer or present me with an inscrutable text to translate. Once I found myself being instructed to take the Bachelor of Hebrew Letters exam required at the end of the fourth year. Very calmly I explained that I had already passed the B.H.L., I had made a point of it before enlisting in the Merchant Marine. No matter, you must take the exam. My explanation grew less cogent, more fevered. No matter, you must take the exam. And so on.

Sometimes my father was present in the dreams, mostly not. Of course not, I said to myself now, he let you off the hook. Yes, I replied as I started the car and drove around to the rear of the dormitory, *he* let you off the hook.

In my day the few cars owned by students, usually cooperatively, were parked on a cinder-strewn rim overlooking a deep, wooded ravine. I gaped now at the expanse of asphalt, the profusion of stalls neatly defined with whitewash. The amount of landfill alone, how did they ever? They indeed, my dear van Winkle. Half a century.

I looked at once for the window from which my father had called, reminding me of the dinner date we would never keep. It was difficult to locate, half-obscured now behind a forbidding security barrier of chain link and concrete. But I found it.

The loquacious student manager of the dormitory escorted me to the suite I'd be occupying and mustered a particle of interest when I informed him I had once studied at HUC. Things are very different now, he let me know. We're affiliated with the Jewish Institute of Religion in New York, we have a campus in Los Angeles, and all students spend their first year in Jerusalem, mainly in order to obtain a working knowledge of Hebrew. I felt a pang of envy. My father and I, joining battle over the severe columns of conjugations and inflections in Davidson—literally, what a heap of heartache he might have been spared.

I entered the suite, shut the door and looked around, feeling like an intruder. When I first came to the College, the man who lived here was a retired faculty member, a famous Talmudist. He had taught my father, and soon after I arrived, I was taken to meet him. The room smelled of old books and an aging man. He had a white beard; behind gold-rimmed spectacles his eyes were bright blue and spirited, but I had the feeling they weren't really seeing me. "Ah yes," he said when we were introduced. "Ah yes." Which is what he repeated whenever we met after that, never more, never less.

I walked to a window. The weather was clearing. A brisk wind scattered leaves off the oaks and elms dotting the slopes of the ravine. I could see the backs of the mansions lining Clifton Avenue. They had been put up during Cincinnati's heyday as a colorful riverboat port, but by the time I arrived at HUC many had been converted to student housing for the University.

A girl I went out with before I met Lee had roomed in one of the residences. The painted red brick looked the same, the masonry trim preserved in the exact crumbly state I remembered. Rita was from the Deep South, slow and sweet and pretty. My father took us out to dinner on one of his visits to Cincinnati, and I watched him charm her. Rita told me later, shaking her head in languid wonderment, "He made me feel like there was no other woman in the world but me, no woman ever."

I wondered how he had acted when he first met Selma, who was not at all slow, probably not too sweet, and always appeared briskly confident of her exotic beauty. Had there been a mutually perceived thunderbolt, a nanosecond in which both love and destiny were revealed? Had my mother been there when they first set eyes on each other?

All at once I felt chilled and weary. I wondered just how smart an idea it was to be travelling this road. But I had begun the journey, and I had just enough of my father's stubbornness — and my mother's — not to turn back.

I left the ancient scholar's suite and climbed to the third floor. The corridors seemed the same, narrower of course, but I was ready for that, almost everyone who returns to earlier haunts speaks of the time-shrinkage effect. I half-expected to see Jasper, the mostly silent, faintly creepy houseman who collected our laundry once a week and occasionally drove a vacuum cleaner through our rooms. Then I was standing outside a pair of doors midway along the hall. One had opened into the study I shared with my roommate Randy — four-walled with books, two desks precisely centered and facing each other. The first couple of years, when we were taking undergraduate and graduate courses simultaneously, we seldom closed our books before two a.m., and then only because of exhaustion or ferocious hunger, or both. If the workload was desperate, we'd haul out a strictly forbidden hotplate and fry up greasy collations (which fortunately with time became a mite more refined) while we continued our bulldozer attack on The Song of Songs or some sly morality tale from the Midrash. More often we walked down the hill, passing the vast, cool facade of the Good Samaritan Hospital to reach an intersection HUC students called the Short Corner. There we'd onload intemperate amounts of torrid Cincinnati chili blizzarded with minced raw onion. Up the hill again, to sleep a few hours and wake at six to cram in another hour or two at our desks before racing three-quarters of a mile up Clifton Avenue toward the Long Corner and our first U. of C. class of the day.

It was also strictly forbidden to have female guests on the upper floors of the dorm, but we'd manage to sneak our steady girlfriends upstairs during the afternoon or evening we took off each week. Scheduling of heavy-necking time in the bedroom was both intricate and delicate.

The day my father died, I didn't cry. Nor did I later, during the long Sunday night when Lee, Randy and I drove through miles of pea-soup fog in the mountains on our way to Baltimore. Nor the next night, when I stood alone in candlelight before his open coffin and gazed at the rouged cheeks and the motionless eyelids and the dark hair carefully slicked back from the widow's peak.

Nor ever for six months, until one evening, inside the room whose door I was staring at now, lying beside Lee on the bed, I started to cry, couldn't stop, and for hours wept in her arms.

* * *

One of the places I liked best at HUC was the Bumming Room. During the day when we had a few minutes off we could always find someone there to hang out with. We lolled across the worn, comfortable leather chairs and sofas and kibitzed while we read our mail or waited to use the pay phone. At night the room was warmly lighted, and after our meal we'd usually linger for gossip and horseplay before heading off to study. Sometimes a celebrity scheduled to lecture at the University would come for dinner and afterward talk to us informally in the Bumming Room. I recall Sinclair Lewis, looking a little like a peeled fetus, and certainly pickled in alcohol, baiting us with a succession of caustic observations about the Jews of small town America. We sat paralyzed for a few outraged and incredulous beats before erupting en masse. Lewis threw back his bald, mottled head and cackled until he nearly choked.

The old warm, sprawling Bumming Room was no more. It had been partitioned into a warren of rectangles and trapezoids, the most inviting of which suggested a motel lobby designed by someone named Polly Prim. A woman in her early twenties was seated on one of the straight-backed sofas, books and notepads fanned out around her. I had heard that the student body still numbered less than a hundred, but now more than a quarter were women. I thought about some of the professors who would not yet have died or retired by the time the College sidled toward admitting women. I could imagine their dudgeon at the idea of a female voice reading from the Talmud in a classroom, let alone preaching from a pulpit. I nodded to the young woman, who eyed me suspiciously over the top of her glasses as I turned and walked toward the dining room.

I had expected it to be different, so I wasn't disappointed. Only vaguely saddened. Cafeteria rails along two walls and rows of long messhall eating surfaces had replaced the round, damask-draped, tastefully spaced tables I recalled.

In the 1930s a quirky philanthropist ignored pleas for a contribution to the College's hard-pressed academic program and endowed a fund that had to be spent exclusively on the students' living facilities. Moreover, the money had to be entirely disbursed during his lifetime. He was not young. We of course never questioned the reason for his animus. We dined well off good china, served by black waiters in white jackets. A number of our fellow students had fled Germany early in the decade. Some were religiously more conservative than we mainstream American Reform Jews, so while the dietary laws were not slavishly observed, no obvious *traif* such as pork or shellfish came to the table. The Europeans also brought with them the custom of chanting the blessings before and after meals, which soon became part of our routine. The melodies were lovely. At a certain stage in my HUC career I had made a point of spurning the ritual. I was glad I could recall it now with pleasure.

I crossed the dining room to a set of double doors and peered through a circular window at what I'd really come to see. If we students wanted something to eat before the set breakfast hour, we could fetch coffee and toast from the kitchen. One morning a few months after my father died, as I was filling a cup from the giant urn, I heard someone call me. I turned to see a young man with dark wavy hair and aquiline features. I knew him well.

Jonah was a recent graduate of the College. He had been appointed assistant rabbi at Har Sinai the year before my father resigned to become head of the Union. Until that year my father had somehow escaped public censure for his affair with Selma. I'm certain this was due in part to the efforts of a number of his devoted followers in the congregation, though how they managed it in those times still puzzles me. Soon after Jonah arrived, scandal began to smoulder. I believed then that he vigorously fanned each spark, more out of ambition than probity. My conviction was hardly objective, but it was decidedly fierce.

I tried to recapture the feel and texture of that moment. Jonah smiling, hand outstretched. Randy was there. He told me afterward that my face went bloodless, and he was sure I was going to plow into Jonah. But after a few seconds I turned abruptly away. Later, a pacifist upper-classman who had also witnessed the incident lectured me on the grave spiritual consequences of harboring such hatred.

For an unexpected instant all that hatred surged back. I wanted to kill. Then my rage abated. A leavening question: What was I defending?

* * *

I must have looked a little spooky when I returned to the truncated Bumming Room. The student on the sofa frowned, tightened the circle of books around her tucked-up legs and inquired icily if she could help me. I was considering a reply that began well Rabbi since you asked, when Randy and Edna walked in. The student blinked at our noisy greetings and frowned more deeply.

Rabbi Randall Falk had spent over a quarter of a century as leader of the Nashville, Tennessee Reform congregation and had recently retired to teach and write. After I left the College we lost each other for a while, but that got remedied, and now we met a time or two a year. This reunion was special. Randy knew why I was in Cincinnati, and he timed a research trip of his own to coincide. He had worshipped my father; we planned to talk.

He was originally from Little Rock, Arkansas. Elocution instruction was required when we were students, and a substantial elderly lady with bristling white chin whiskers labored diligently to rectify Randy's drawl and my Maryland mushmouth. "From the diaphragm, from the dia-phragm," she would intone, seizing our hands and guiding them to a spot just below her promontory of a bosom. "Listen to the way I say it. And feel. Feel!" The layers of flesh shuddered and heaved like a giant bellows. "What do the gentlemen wish?" she would cry in ascending tones. "What do they want?"

Randy's return to the South eradicated most of our teacher's influence on him. Now, whenever he and I spend an evening together, we seem to provoke each other to progressive diction deterioration. Gloria, my wife, swears that after our third glass of wine, it's impossible to understand a word either of us is saying.

Randy and I came to the College at 18, imbued with New Deal liberal-ism. We moved impetuously and naively farther left. Often, instead of getting the sleep we badly needed, we'd lie awake in the darkness, talking excitedly about what we hoped to accomplish in the rabbinate. We shared doubts and crises of belief. I succumbed to mine. Randy subjugated his, and modelled his ministry after my father's. He was in the vanguard on social issues. Like my father, he had for some time chaired the Social Justice Commission of the Central Conference of American Rabbis. He slugged away for civil rights at the grass roots level long before it became fashionable. He was an eloquent advocate on the interfaith circuit. He also grew more genuinely devoted to Jewish ritual. It could have become a point of contention between us. We kept it muted.

From watching my mother, I knew how intolerably a congregation can importune a rabbi's wife. Often they'll nip at her heels when they can't get at the rabbi. Even when a rabbi is beloved and beyond conventional criticism, congregations may still fasten a "Caesar's wife" label on his spouse. Edna Falk had coped well. She had intelligence, patience and humor, the tools of a class diplomat.

I found myself thinking now that Gloria, despite her Methodist-Presbyterian background, might have made an excellent rabbi's wife. Qualification was one thing, inclination quite another. She would have been appalled at the prospect of inhabiting any manse, regardless of denomination. I wondered if I dared phone her to say my re-visiting Cincinnati had excited a conversion, and I was planning to resume my rabbinical career. I decided maybe I'd already teased her enough by constantly insisting her mother had to be Jewish, because only a Jew could be so anti-Semitic.

The student on the sofa suddenly sat up straight, her scowl giving way to a warm smile. I turned to see Dr. Marcus entering the room. He was dressed entirely in black — severely tailored suit, cape-coat and a broad-brimmed hat. Somehow the striking ensemble seemed in no way affected. He walked slowly but firmly, leaning on a heavy walking stick.

We shook hands and held on, looking into each other's eyes. My father's friend, I was thinking, and later mine. If my father had lived, I was thinking, this was the way he'd look now: concentric pouches beneath teary eyes, age spots, a fretwork of wrinkles. I'd have been watching him reach this stage; but if we had met frequently enough, I probably wouldn't have even noticed how he was aging until maybe one day I'd have said to myself with sad pride: my father's old. In the meantime, I was thinking, he'd have been there.

I didn't know what Dr. Marcus was thinking while we clasped each other's hands. But suddenly he smiled, and suddenly looked years younger. "Welcome back," he said.

In the car he issued Randy running instructions through a labyrinth of streets, directing us toward his favorite fish restaurant. Randy had been Dr. Marcus' secretary when we were students. They'd remained close. Randy asked a question. "I've already told you the answer to that," Dr. Marcus replied. "You can't remember anything anymore." He peered at Randy. "I believe you're getting senile."

He loved to gossip. He'd lived away from his native West Virginia for nearly 75 years, but his twangy drawl was still pure Appalachia. He began telling us a story, about a rabbi he had no time for. He spent several minutes relating in salty detail how the rabbi had made a special idiot of himself. "Of course," he concluded, "I can't document a word of this, not a single footnote." He smiled beatifically. "Furthermore, I don't intend to. When I'm a scientist, I'm a scientist. When I'm a bastard, I'm a bastard."

* * *

In one of the letters Dr. Marcus had written me, he'd listed a number of key words to use as aide-memoires when we got together to talk about my father. The morning after our dinner we'd been sitting in the study of his house for about an hour and had progressed through about half the list. He was relating how early in their HUC career my father had been the class's outstanding scholar. "It was my greatest ambition to beat him, but I never could, not as long as he wanted to stay on top. Then, I don't know what happened, but around the end of his fourth year, suddenly he wasn't interested in Hebrew studies any more. From then on, Eddie seemed to have developed a different agenda." He grinned. "Anyhow, I didn't mind. From then on, I was the star." "Do you think," I asked, "that might have been when he started getting involved in social action?"

"I doubt it. We were pretty young still, what, nineteen, twenty years old. My guess is he was getting restless. Don't ask me why. We knew each other well, but we didn't share too many secrets."

We talked about my father's prowess at tennis, my grandparents, the crystal sets my Uncle Dorman was perpetually putting together in the basement of the family house, how Emma always seemed to be playing one of her sons against the other.

We talked about my father's politics, his close ties to the Roosevelt White House. "There's no question in my mind that your dad would have become one of the most influential American Jewish leaders of our century. And I'll tell you something else. I'm convinced he never did anything for personal glory. He fought for things he believed in. He didn't just pontificate on social justice in the Bible the way most rabbis do. If Eddie thought he was right about something, he'd put his ass on the line, never mind the consequences." He paused, looking down at his hands.

I glanced at my list. "Women," I said.

Dr. Marcus leaned back in his chair. "You have to be aware of the time we lived in. We were very inexperienced. I truly believe that while we were students, everybody in our class was a virgin. Everybody, that is, except Eddie."

My father had apparently gone for some time with one girl who was crazy about him, but left her to begin a wild romance with the sister of a classmate. Everyone expected them to marry, but my father backed away amid an uproar that eventually involved the HUC faculty.

"I never condemned him," Dr. Marcus said. "Eddie was his own person, and if he decided not to marry, he must have had a reason, and that was his business. Actually — again remembering the times — I think it took considerable courage for him to do what he did. But the way he didn't give a damn what people thought or said, sometimes he carried it too far. In Baltimore he had an affair with a woman named Mrs. Gordon."

"I know about that," I said. "But I think you've got the name wrong."

"I never get names wrong."

I mentioned Selma's last name. Dr. Marcus shook his head. "Mrs. Gordon," he repeated, and started to describe her position in the Baltimore Jewish community, the organizations she had belonged to.

I interrupted him. "I knew Mrs. Gordon. When was all this supposed to be happening, do you know?"

"Of course I know. The mid-1920s."

"Oh," I said, relieved. "That may have been."

"Not may have been," Dr. Marcus said. "Was."

* * *

I stood next to my car outside Dr. Marcus' house, which occupied a high corner on a quiet street not far from the College. The municipality had renamed the intersection Marcus Square, declared his house a monument and painted it a striking crimson and blue.

In a few minutes I was supposed to return to the College and start looking at the collection of my father's papers, but I was dragging my feet, more upset by what I'd just heard from Dr. Marcus than I wanted to admit.

To the best of my knowledge, Selma and my father had begun their affair around 1928 or '29. I may have learned about it soon after it started through my father's anguished outpourings in the car, but those memories were subliminal and unreliable. Certainly, though, by the mid-30s, when I was in my teens, I'd half-overheard enough of my parents' late-night quarrels to suspect the relationship had been going on for quite a while. And after I entered HUC, my father confirmed it. He told me quietly that he cared a great deal for my mother, but he loved Selma more. He was aware, he said, that in his position it should never have happened. But it had, and he would have to find a way of resolving the situation. He didn't have to add the obvious. In those days a congregation might barely have tolerated a rabbi and his wife separating amicably. A messy parting would inevitably have resulted in dismissal. This splitup — considering the fact that Selma was also married — would have become instantly infamous.

I had been fond of my mother, and desperately sorry for her, but sometimes also angry. I remember feeling when I was in my teens that if my father loved Selma and no longer loved my mother, it would be less painful for her if she let him go. I thought then that Great Love conquered all, without much sense of what love was, never mind the modifier.

I had always been able to accept my father's love for Selma. Yet in Dr. Marcus' study, for a brief moment I'd been confronted with a cheapening of that love, and so a devaluation of my image of my father.

And even now that I'd got the time frame straight, I was still disturbed. And annoyed with myself for being disturbed. So the old man got it on with Roberta Gordon before Selma, I told myself, big deal, at least he kept them in sequence, and you with *your* stellar track record, you're going to throw rocks at papa? I sighed. There was no way I was going to get to the Archives that afternoon.

* * *

I couldn't find a trace of the Forest Theatre. Nor of the soda fountain where Paden used to take me after the show, though both had still existed in 1939 when I first came to the College. Now there was a clump of anonymous brick buildings.

So I was surprised when I turned onto Reading Road and found a number of the old apartment houses still intact. The dingy grey facade behind which my mother's parents had existed ignominiously for a time after the demise of my grandmother's "hotel". And a few blocks further on, a yellow-brick low-rise, one of the many dwellings where Paden and Emma had lighted briefly during her restless ricochets around the neighborhood.

One classic change. Along this whole section of Reading Road, once the nucleus of a flourishing Jewish community, I saw practically no white faces. When the Jews move out, the blacks move in. Cycles of deprivation and upward mobility, the exposed edges of the migrations grinding against one another like tectonic plates.

It was starting to look like rain again as I parked in front of the house where Lee had lived. I remembered how her father disliked me. He was an observant Jew who had no use for anyone connected with the College.

He had been born in Odessa and still retained a thick accent, but his English was fluent, even sharp. He scratched out a living by jobbing lots of miscellaneous *shmates* around Ohio, Indiana and Kentucky. The house was shabby then. It had changed remarkably little; white paint still peeled from its weathered frame.

A young black man came out onto the porch and stood where Lee and I had kissed and shivered through winters of protracted goodnights. The man sat down on a step without taking his eyes off me. I started the car. For the second time since I had arrived in the city I was ready to give up. What was the point of grubbing through a tangle of youthful roots when I wasn't even sure what I was looking for? And when whatever I did manage to discover only depressed or vexed me. I was even becoming uneasy about what the Archives might turn up. Better just to forget the whole thing, go back to Toronto and start working on a novel or one of the screenplays I was incubating.

Now that I was here, though, I thought I might take just one quick peek at the Dryer Hotel. It had been a huge old grey stone pile with a porticoed front, falling apart when my grandmother bought it before the First World War, spruced it up and converted it to a residential hostelry, really a glorified boarding house.

We had spent a lot of summers there, staying in a suite on the third floor. Everything about it was a small child's paradise. No matter how often I explored the dark-paneled halls with their flowered carpeting and the steep, murky back stairways, I always seemed to be venturing into thrilling new territory. Black servants fussed over my brother and me, spoiling us to mutual delight. My grandmother set what many called the finest table in Cincinnati. I remember monster haunches of beef opening out beneath the carver's knife like great ruby flowers. There were fresh tongues bathed in a piquant raisin sauce, platters of crispy fried chicken, heaps of corn and okra and spicy pureed yams, and my grandmother's special potato salad, made with caraway seed and a tingly mustard dressing. Not to mention the cakes — a dozen choices at each meal, dense and creamy or flaky and ephemeral. And for a grace note — God knows how in those days she got them live to inland Cincinnati — she even served whole steamed lobsters once a week.

I played catch with my father on the front lawn. Outside the back door, a black kitchen helper named Clyde taught me how to turn the handle of the ice cream freezer, and some Fridays when he produced the supply for the week, he'd let me chill one whole batch all by myself. "Turn her slow, turn her easy," he'd croon. "Don't nothin' get there sweeter for travelin' fast."

I saw my first corpse in the Dryer Hotel. A woman tenant dropped dead. A couple of men carried her to her room and laid her on the bed. The doctor came and left. I crept in later and stood beside her, poised to run, feeling a delicious fear ebb and flow.

My father taught me how to play rummy. Sometimes he and my mother and I would sit in the commodious, dourly furnished front room before dinner, laughing and slapping down cards on the table, while famished guests eddied around us, sniffing furtively at the delectable smells wafting under the closed door of the dining room.

My grandmother could never bear to charge people what she should have. Nor could she press tenants who fell behind in their rent. In time, inevitably, she went broke.

I drove up and down Reading Road, unable to find the hotel. Finally, after I got a proper fix on a couple of landmarks, I understood why. Where the building had stood was now a weed-choked lot. All that remained familiar was the enormous spreading oak that had shaded the stone stoop at the rear of the hotel where I once turned the handle of the ice cream freezer.

I got out of the car and picked my way through a snarl of wet grass and browning goldenrod, wondering what I was doing. It started to rain.

Then without even a forewarning, as I stood there getting soaked under that dreary November sky, I could feel myself beginning to grow excited. About why I was in Cincinnati, about stirring up the past, seeking. I even felt—I could hardly believe it—something oddly akin to joy.

* * *

There were six large boxes. Kevin, the amiable but somewhat laconic young archivist, had to make several trips to get them all to the table where I was unlimbering writing materials. When they were finally assembled, they looked like fortifications around my workspace. For which almost at once I was to be unexpectedly grateful.

The documents seemed to be classified more by category than chronology, so I opened a box at random. The first thing that caught my eye was a folder bearing my name. It contained a number of my letters to my mother from Germany, where I had worked with the United Nations for five years after the War. These were dated over the spring and summer of 1947, when my first marriage was falling apart. I could only get through a few of them before closing the folder, chagrined.

I remembered that my mother had sent a batch of papers to the Archives about twenty years before. I hunkered down lower in my chair, trying not to imagine how many eyes had pored over those mortifying words since. I glanced around. A cool-looking young woman with a mane of tawny hair gazed fixedly past me from a nearby table, tapping her cheek with a pen. I grew certain that she had read every word of my letters and that her faint, abstracted smile was really knowingly sardonic.

My paranoia evaporated pretty rapidly. Irritation with my mother took longer. Why had she gone public with my highly personal letters without my permission, without even telling me? Was this the fruit of some long-hoarded resentment, her way of getting even because I had so clearly been my father's son? I decided that wasn't it because I didn't want it to be.

I went to Kevin's office. "I've found some personal papers of mine," I began.

"And you'd like them restricted."

I gave him a sharp glance. Had *he* read the letters? "Yes please," I breathed. "The folder's under my name."

"No problem. Happens all the time." He grinned. "Done."

I returned to the boxes. I knew I'd be able only to browse through them this trip, and that was fine. I had to visit Baltimore. I needed to talk to my brother in Los Angeles, and also to try to locate Lee, who I knew was living there. I wanted to track down Marge, Selma's daughter. Then I'd come back here.

It wasn't difficult to turn up examples of my father's feisty style. PUBLIC WANTS BACK-SLAPPING GAS BAGS, NOT INTELLECTUAL CLERGY, RABBI SAYS, ran a 1927 Baltimore Sun headline.

When the Nazi battleship *Emden* scheduled a visit to Baltimore in 1936, the mayor and governor fell over themselves planning elaborate welcoming festivities. My father tore into them savagely, only to be attacked in turn by influential members of his congregation, who felt it was "not the time to stir up trouble among the gentiles".

Once again my father put his job on the line. Once again he won his congregational battle, this time with the help of a special cadre, a group of men and women he had inspired over the years with his principles of social action and his courage in fighting for them. There were maybe thirty of them, mostly my father's age, but one was in his seventies. Some were wealthy, a few pretty nearly dirt-poor. All had become close personal friends. They would have walked through fire for my father, and in time many of them did.

The city and state feted the personnel of the *Emden* as planned, but my father's rampage made the high public officials uncomfortable. The mayor sent an emissary to my father's office to find out "how mad he was." My father was mad.

Riffling through papers, I found a sermon, again from 1936. One sentence grabbed my attention. "Between them," my father stated all those years ago, "the right and left will destroy democracy."

I didn't remember the sermon, possibly hadn't even heard it. Nor could I recall any specific conversations we'd had on the subject. I was aware, though, of how vehemently he fought political extremists. And twenty years after he delivered the sermon I was holding in my hand, I had made its central statement the theme for my first published novel. Would I have got there on my own?

I came across references to High Holyday positions he had held while he was at the College. Every year the entire student body would be dispersed over Rosh Hashonah and Yom Kippur to towns too small to support even a bi-weekly pulpit. Mainly they were in the South: Louisiana, Alabama, Oklahoma, Texas. Almost all these Jewish communities had been founded around the turn of the century by immigrant peddlers who for one reason or another chose a particular location to sink roots. My father ministered to these early patriarchs and their growing clans. By the time I became a student rabbi, a few of the old lions were still alive, and when they were, there was no question who ruled the den. But my congregants consisted mostly of their offspring.

I was never sent to a town where my father had officiated, but there was a likeness that endured over time and distance. He and I used to mix and match stories about our High Holyday jobs. Almost all the pillars of the community were retailers of some sort—department, drug or hardware stores. There was at that time only a sprinkling of lawyers and doctors. The older generation had European accents; their children usually sounded as if they'd lived forever on a diet of corn pone and collard greens. This wasn't new to me. My fraternity brothers at Chapel Hill had been great y'allers. I had visited their homes in small towns of the Carolinas and Tennessee. However, it was a different matter arriving in a southern community as a spiritual leader.

The moment we stepped off the train or bus we were addressed as "Rabbi", which especially on a maiden voyage was pretty heady stuff for us callow shepherds. But that was just the beginning. Sometimes by the end of the second day, rarely later then the third, an almost imperceptible promotion would take place and suddenly our flocks would begin calling us "Doctor".

The women had been cooking for weeks, and the student rabbi would be the table decoration at a progression of sumptuous meals, some savory, some that sank to the pit of the stomach like petrified gefillte fish. Gluttony was encouraged, even required, and while we were trying to cope with its consequences, we were expected to address gatherings of the Rotary and Kiwanis. The local press solicited and magnified our opinions. And through all this wove the parade of marriageable daughters, each cheered on by a mama extolling her beauty and skills.

Still, there were often memorable moments during those two weeks. Walking at twilight with a young couple past the outskirts of the town, onto the vastness of the prairie, listening to their ambitions, their worries. Standing in the pulpit on the eve of the Day of Atonement, looking out over the faces of the fifty or sixty people seated in rows on folding chairs in the Masonic Lodge auditorium. Hearing the proprietor of Finkelstein's Variety Store sing the *Kol Nidre*. Gaining a sense of what it meant to be this kind of stranger, one of few among the many, where you knew from unalterable experience that underneath all the jocular Main Street cameraderie lurked endemic suspicion.

I rummaged through more papers in the collection and came on a letter written midway through the Great War by the University of Cincinnati's President, warmly supporting my father's application to become an artillery officer. I learned later from Fran that the Army had rejected him because of a heart murmur, but she had no idea why he had wanted to give up his theological studies — and the draft deferment that went with them — to enlist for combat. He never mentioned it to me, though by 1941 he knew the same intention was hanging around, muted for the moment, at the base of my skull. Maybe the omission was deliberate. He wanted me to be a rabbi, no question of that. Maybe he felt that in fairness he had to offer me freedom of choice, which he did, graciously. But no way was he going to build a fire under it.

The Hunger Marchers article came to light, but my understanding of what it meant escaped me then. In fact, while I sat reading it in the Archives, I found myself experiencing an instant of childish disappointment that my father really hadn't driven that taxi loaded with food through a hail of machine gun fire.

The summer of 1941. His appointment as Union head and the deluge of congratulatory messages. The Mayor of Baltimore and the Governor of Maryland, both penning flowery praise, both no doubt ecstatic to finally be rid of him. Congressmen, Senators, a letter from Roosevelt, one from the warden of the Baltimore City Jail beginning "Dear Doc", a note in near-illegible handwriting from Supreme Court Justice Frankfurter.

That same summer of 1941, Selma's husband died suddenly. They were vacationing on the other side of Maine from us. I drove my father across the state to their cottage. I remember even now my mother's expression as she stood on the porch watching us get into the car. When we arrived, my father disappeared with Selma. Her daughter Marge and I hung about together, a pair of disconsolate waifs smoking like twin chimneys, silently skipping stones across the surface of the lake.

Now on cue, a letter in the Archives from Marge, written a couple of months before that day, telling my father how happy she was about his new job.

A number of letters like, "I'll always remember you for the great kindness you did me a few years ago." One from, according to the letterhead, a Manufacturer of Straw and Felt Hats: "You probably don't realize the profound influence upon my character and life knowing you has caused. That sounds jumbled, but I think you will know what I mean."

And then a stapled sheaf of papers I held for a long moment before beginning to read. It was headed *Union of American Hebrew Congregations, Proceedings of the Executive Board, Cincinnati, Ohio, October 19, 1941.* I turned the pages. The trivia of meetings, the droning, the petty bickering, the elaborate courtesy masking subterfuge and hostility. My father accommodating, maneuvering, attacking, dealing all that long morning and into the afternoon. And as I read, I was suffocatingly aware, moment by moment, of the obstruction narrowing his arteries, the infarct forming. My father got up to speak. He was about to make his case for moving the Union to Washington, into the mainstream. "I could not have risen on a matter that concerns me more deeply," he began. "I ask you (to believe) that what I'm going to say to you is devoid of any ulterior motives (and that I am) speaking the truth as I feel it in the depth of my heart."

I turned the page. Naturally, I knew what was coming, but even half a century later I still wasn't ready for it. "At this point," the minutes dispassionately noted, "Rabbi Israel was stricken with a heart attack and passed away instantly."

The table, the boxes blurred. I had to get out of there.

* * *

There was a nip in the air, but the sun was benign, the yellowing leaves touched with russet, the kind of Cincy fall weather I liked to remember. Randy and I walked toward the Long Corner, as we had hundreds of times all those years ago. Randy loved food, he'd put on some weight, and I guess I wasn't exactly emaciated myself. But we still enjoyed walking fast, and enjoyed knowing we still could. We zipped along, chatting casually, now and then snagging a memory. Riding horses across his cousin's cotton farm in central Arkansas. Hitching rides with truckers through steamy Mississippi darkness, skipping sleep so we could get to New Orleans faster and gorge on oysters and shrimp gumbo.

Without mentioning it we veered away from the U. of C. campus, but not because we couldn't bear the changes. True, it was a hustling factory now, chrome and glass crammed into every available corner. And there was certainly a degree of nostalgia for when we studied Shakespeare and Whitman and Beowulf in musty lecture halls where the floors and desks creaked and the professors knew our names. But we had never been emotionally rooted in the University the way we were in HUC. Still, we were relieved when we turned toward Burnet Woods and found the winding paths much the same as when we had brought our books there on warm spring days.

I told Randy what I'd learned from Dr. Marcus about my father's involvement with another woman before Selma. "Are you sure you can handle all this?" he asked.

I said I hoped so. But without wanting to I was recalling an image from *Death of a Salesman*, Willy's adolescent son witnessing his father's adultery. I dismissed it briskly. I'm not Biff Loman, I thought. And even if I have had illusions about my father, I'm past seventy for God's sake, sure, I can handle it.

Randy looked as if he was about to say something cautionary. But he didn't, and we talked about what it meant to lose your father when you were in your early twenties, after you'd got old enough to be truly aware of him but not yet at an age when you were subconsciously starting to anticipate his death. Randy's father died a few years after mine, "just when we were beginning to understand each other". We agreed it could be like an amputation. At times for the rest of your life you'll suddenly feel the limb is still there. Only it's not.

We talked a bit about Randy's children—three, and at that point a couple of grandchildren. I've always considered it lucky for everyone actually or potentially involved that my first two marriages produced no offspring. Gloria and I have known each other for more than thirty years, but by the time we discovered we were in love and wanted to live together, it was too late to have kids. I get along well with her son Michael, who's in his forties, but he has a father, and his approach to me is more friendly than filial, which we both find preferable to a show of ritual posturing. Sometimes Gloria and I regret we didn't get together earlier, but we agree it was never time until it was time. And we don't consider not having children of our own a calamity. But now, doing what I was doing, the question occurred: does not having a child color the way a man looks at his own father?

Randy reminded me of a car trip he had taken with my father shortly before his death. My father was scheduled for an evening lecture in Indianapolis, and Randy had to be in nearby Kokomo, his bi-weekly congregation, at the same time. Randy drove my father to the hall where he was speaking, and they made arrangements to go back to Cincinnati together later that night.

My father drove the return leg. His way with an automobile always made any passengers aware of life's evanescence, and this may have put Randy in a confessional mood. He told my father he had always hoped that one day he could be his assistant. Since my father would no longer be ministering to a congregation, this was now of course impossible. Randy had had to set new sights, he told my father, and this was causing a lot of old doubts and some new ones to surface. He went on to speak about things he had never discussed with anyone. My father, hell-bent along the road to Cincinnati, seemed to maintain a center of quiet in himself. "I've never known anyone to listen the way he did. You wanted to keep talking, you wanted to tell him absolutely everything, and you felt he wanted to hear it. He'd ask a question now and then, but otherwise he just listened. He *listened*. The loss I felt when he died, it was terrible."

We all—Randy, Lee and I—almost added to the loss the night my father died. All three of us were under pretty much strain on the long trek east. Randy and I spelled each other driving, and once (Randy was recalling now) while he was at the wheel, all of us fell asleep. He didn't know what woke him, but he jammed on the brake to find the car on one of those hairpin mountain turns, inches short of a sheer, seemingly bottomless dropoff.

We circled out of Burnet Woods, heading for the Short Corner. It looked a lot as it had when we were students, but our chili parlor local had vanished, replaced by a bar that hinted genteely — this being a virtuous section of the city — at live entertainment with "girls". However, there was a chain establishment nearby whose chili, Randy promised, wasn't too bad.

We ordered jumbo portions over spaghetti along with chili dogs smothered in raw onions and cheese. "I remember one night," Randy said while we were waiting, "you were called to the phone. When you came back to the room, your face was like a sheet." Randy, it would seem, had watched me go pale quite a lot. "The call was from your father. It was the spring of 1940, Hitler had invaded the Low Countries a week or so before, and Dave Niles had just phoned your father."

David Niles was one of Roosevelt's political advisors and a close friend of our family. He was a slight, taciturn man who moved in a shroud of cigarette smoke and could have served as a model for Alec Guiness' later portrayal of Smiley. He could be genial. When Randy and I visited him in his White House office earlier in the year, he took us on a behind-the-scenes tour. We ended up in the Oval Office, which Roosevelt had left only minutes before. Dave encouraged us each to sit for a moment in the President's chair, which delighted us. When he spoke to my father on this particular night, however, he was apparently not so genial.

Nor was my father. "Sometimes I wonder where you hide your brains," he fulminated. "Do you have any idea what your stupidity could do to your rabbinical career?" I didn't even try to ask what it was all about. When he was on this kind of warpath, he would get to what was bothering him in his own good time. Which was invariably my bad time.

This time he got to the bottom line pretty fast. Randy and I had signed our names to an anti-war letter originated by a group on the FBI's list of communist-front organizations. My father hated communists, and most particularly the American brand. He felt they were ruthless, reckless and wrong-headed. He resigned from at least two associations when he became convinced they were communist-manipulated. Yet on many occasions he publicly defended the Soviet Union against right-wing vituperation. And only a month after the night Randy was referring to, he let me voice from his pulpit my opposition to America's involvement in the War.

But that was later. While I was listening to his voice lash out over the phone that night, I had some sense of how the Mayor of Baltimore and the Governor of Maryland had felt on various occasions, and maybe even how King Zedekiah might have reacted when Jeremiah really got on his case.

Our food arrived. Randy picked up his chili dog and grinned. "Boy, were you shook up that night."

"And you weren't after I passed on the message he told me to give *you*?"

Randy threw me a look and took an enormous bite of chili dog. "I sure wish," he said, "I could still eat the way we used to."

* * *

It was late Friday afternoon and raining again. I was driving back to Toronto early the next morning, so I phoned Dr. Marcus to thank him and say goodbye. He asked if I wanted to drop by the house. I found him stretched out on the couch in his study, looking a little tired. In a few minutes the widow of a former student would turn up to drive him to the College, where he always attended Friday evening services in the chapel. We talked quietly about a variety of things — the days when I was at the College, his memories of his father, whom he referred to as "a West Virginia dirt farmer", the current international situation.

Dr. Marcus' wife had died years ago, and he never remarried. His only child, a singer, was killed in her early thirties in a Los Angeles hotel fire. He was alone, but probably only sporadically lonely and not at all sorry for himself. His work energized and fulfilled him. His four-volume history of the American Jews would soon be coming out, one volume a year. He intended, he said now, to live at least long enough to see them all published.

"Did your dad believe in a personal God?" he asked abruptly.

I had puzzled over this and still wasn't sure of the answer. "I think so," I said finally.

"I don't," he said. A twinge of bitterness around his mouth and eyes, quickly gone. "I doubt many rabbis do."

Hilda arrived and let him know she'd be waiting outside. Dr. Marcus tightened his black tie, donned his black coat and hat. We clasped hands and held on for a moment, as we had when we re-met. Then I helped him out through the rain to Hilda's car.

* * *

The rain stopped as I was returning from dinner. I parked the car and walked along the driveway to the foot of the lawn, where I had a full view of both the dormitory and the classroom building.

Mist was drifting up from the ravine. The moist air carried an odor I had always associated with nighttime Cincinnati. We used to joke that the only way Procter and Gamble could make Ivory Soap 99 and 44/100 percent pure was by polluting Cincinnati 100 percent. The air was only mildly caustic now, but I remembered that, walking back up to the College at three a.m., it would often sear our throats more than the chili we'd just eaten.

I looked at the stone steps leading to the door of the classroom building. I could now consider with detachment the discomfort I'd undergone in some of those rooms, and even concede that despite my best efforts I had gained something from the experience. And now I was quietly sure, without guilt or defiance, that I was at last off the rabbinical hook. All those years, why hadn't I come back here before? The answer, obvious enough: until now I hadn't been ready.

I turned back toward the dormitory and located the windows of the second-floor suite my father had been staying in at the time of his death.

I had returned to Cincinnati after the funeral in Baltimore, a few days before my twenty-first birthday. I asked for the key to the suite. It was early evening when I unlocked the door, closed it behind me and switched on a lamp. I could hear the voices of my fellow students in the hall as they headed toward their rooms to study. I walked across the suite. The bed had been made up, but nothing else had been disturbed. My father's dressing gown dangled askew over the back of the chair where he'd flung it. A tie he'd probably thought of wearing, then discarded, lay in a sloppy S on the seat of the chair. Magazines and books were strewn across the desk as I was sure he'd left them, next to an ashtray containing a couple of cigarette butts.

My mother planned to come to Cincinnati in the next few days. I knew she'd want to pack my father's clothes, so I didn't touch them. I did, however, shuffle through every piece of paper in the room. I put two letters aside. One was from my mother, pleading with my father not to break up their marriage. The other was from Selma, looking forward to being with my father soon, and to making plans together for the future. I stared at the letters for another few moments, then put them in my pocket, turned out the light and left the suite.

The next day I walked down to the Short Corner, tore both letters into tiny shreds and deposited them in a trashcan.

Now in the darkness a breeze stirred, soft for autumn. A light went on behind a third-floor window, just above the suite where my father had stayed.

My mama done told me, I sang softly, *when I was in kneepants, my mama done told me*—zip. Nada. Not a word, ever.

FIVE

For most of his long life, my maternal grandfather breathed through a hole cut into his windpipe.

In his late twenties, which would make it around 1890, he was working for the family business, a carriage hire establishment in New York. Somehow — I never got the details quite straight — a carriage fell on my grandfather, paralyzing him, and he nearly suffocated before a doctor arrived and performed an emergency tracheotomy.

Gradually he recovered, sufficiently to father three of his four children, including Amelia, my mother. What finally did him in at the age of 82 was tongue cancer, no doubt encouraged by the foul two for a nickel cigars he smoked steadily through each day. However, for some reason the doctors never closed the incision in his throat. In fact, they gave him a hollow, curved black rubber tube, specially designed to be inserted in the hole and keep it from healing. Wearing a necktie with this contraption would certainly have been awkward, if not painful. So every morning my grandfather tucked a corner of an immaculate white silk handkerchief into the collarless neckband of his shirt and draped it carefully so the mongram — CD for Charles Dryer — was precisely centered between the lapels of his carefully brushed suit coat.

The tube in his throat whistled faintly with each breath, but if this embarrassed him, he never let on. He had great natural dignity, and even when the passage occasionally clogged with fluid, provoking an unnerving phlegmy rattle, he always took courtly time excusing himself before going to change the tube.

After his accident his doctors gravely cautioned him never to work again, an overdire warning as it turned out, but both he and my grandmother accepted the caveat. For a time his lack of gainful employment didn't matter. Charlie Dryer's parents emigrated from England in the 1860s, their transplant shock apparently cushioned by a considerable supply of sterling funds. Enough at any rate for them to occupy a spacious residence on Manhattan's upper East Side and to run a string of racehorses. But the family fortune vanished during one of the turn of the century mini-panics, and suddenly my grandmother had to assume the burden of providing for her husband and four young children.

She was singularly ill-equipped for the task. Not that she lacked accomplishments. She cooked superbly and with incredible speed could transform skeins of yarn into exquisite hooked rugs that might have fetched handsome prices in craft shops.

But like her husband, Josephine Peyser came from a background where money was regarded with disdain simply because there was always plenty of it around. Her grandfather arrived in Charleston, West Virginia from Germany early in the 19th century and prospered in the drygoods business. His son, my great-grandfather, pyramided the initial wealth, then brought the whole edifice down in a flourish of arrogant investments. By this time, though, young Josie was comfortably married to affluent Charlie. Then Charlie's mishap turned that comfort cold.

One of my grandmother's brothers had helped found National Distillers. He died just as he was about to become the corporation's first president, but he did leave Josie a chunk of money. She bundled my grandfather and their brood off to Cincinnati, where one of her sisters lived. Josie borrowed heavily to augment her inheritance and sank everything into her hotel, which in turn eventually sank under the weight of culinary glory and financial ineptitude.

Josie's other brother, my great-uncle Teddy, helped postpone the death throes for a while. He put together a substantial kitty after the First World War and salvaged enough from the 1929 crash to enable him to enter politics. He surfed into the U.S. House of Representatives, representing Manhattan's posh Silk Stocking District, on the crest of Roosevelt's 1932 victory and kept getting re-elected until he died in 1940. Uncle Teddy was neither a terribly energetic nor innovative lawmaker. He was, in fact, an elegant ward-heeler, affably adroit both at raising funds for the Democratic Party and just managing to keep his skirts free of Tammany Hall grime. A bald, rotund, gregarious man, he was happiest hanging out in Congressional cloakrooms and expensive Washington restaurants. My father benefited frequently from his shrewd assessments of Capitol Hill gossip.

Ultimately, even Teddy had to accept that the Dryer Hotel had become little more than a hole to pour money into. The loss of the Reading Road mansion devastated my grandmother. She suffered a couple of mild heart attacks and disconsolately drifted toward invalidism. Charlie was devoted but incapable of looking after her. In those days few children sent their elderly parents to nursing homes. Especially Jewish children. My mother, at the time the most financially secure of the Dryer offspring, was elected to shelter my grandparents. In 1935 they settled into our house in Baltimore.

I shudder now, contemplating the poisonous potential of that move. Basic economics, to begin with. Until 1933, my father's annual salary had been $10,000, plus whatever variable supplements came in from officiating at weddings and funerals, enough in those days to provide a six-bedroom suburban house, two cars and a pair of servants. However, as the Depression deepened, the Har Sinai board whacked a couple thousand off my father's pay. By now his reputation as a speaker was such that he could easily have taken up the slack on the countrywide after-dinner circuit. For a while he did just that, slotting paid appearances at rubber-victual gatherings among freebie addresses and meetings on behalf of the causes he cared about. But his congregational bosses soon vetoed his barnstorming. They were prepared to tolerate his presence at prestigious national events — though, they added, perhaps this too was getting a bit out of hand. But engagements for an honorarium were out. Har Sinai paid him; Har Sinai was entitled to his primary attention. Mindful of my father's temper, they tossed in a softener that was really a sneak-punch. His health was fragile, they reminded him. They wanted him to be their rabbi for many years to come. Yes, they were laying down the law, but surely he realized their firmness was as much in his interest as theirs.

The admonishment contained a certain logic, which my father appeared to recognize. He cancelled all outside bookings for which he was to be paid and substantially curtailed his extra-congregational activities. Within a few months, however, he was once more vigorously involved with all the political and humanitarian organizations he had so obligingly renounced, plus a few new affiliations. I think he expected his board members to challenge him. They didn't. Probably each side considered the standoff a victory. But this didn't alleviate the financial pinch at home, almost certain to be exacerbated by the arrival of my grandparents.

Our house was by no means tiny, but if it had been ten times larger, it still might not have accommodated the tensions between my mother and father. Their struggle was never overtly physical; nobody got bashed or flung about. Nor did they even scream at each other. But there was a low, carrying intensity to their voices. In my bedroom directly above theirs I couldn't help but follow most of their operatic squabbles, as well as the passionate arias of reconciliation that sporadically ensued. My grandparents' beds lay even closer, separated from my mother and father only by an uninsulated wall.

From the moment they met, Josie had never been fond of my father. She was a taciturn woman, but her sparse observations could sometimes be barbed. My mother had a difficult time giving birth to me. It was before the fashion of rampant Caesarians, so I was delivered by forceps, and in the process my head got somewhat squashed. A short time later, my father and grandmother came to look at me. They stood silently for a moment, gazing down at my bloody, misshapen face. Then Josie said brightly, "Looks just like you, Ed."

I got that story from my father. Which I suppose is part of the reason the enforced coexistence didn't work out as calamitously as it might have. He knew Josie had always disliked him, and now in these claustrophobic quarters she had even greater reason to disapprove. But he was also aware that she was a proud woman who had tried valiantly to succeed in a cherished venture. She had not only failed, she was reduced to bitter dependency. On my father, her enemy. He never pretended affection, but in time he began to jolly her. There was respect in the way he teased, even a modicum of warmth. And finally, ever so rarely, she would give him a thin, flickering, but genuine smile.

Then, on an oppressively muggy Rosh Hashonah evening I sat next to her in the sanctuary of the venerable Bolton Street Temple. For generations the surrounding neighborhood had been solidly Jewish, but by now it had begun to conform with the classic pattern: Negroes replacing Jews. Most of the earlier residents had moved north, toward the Pikesville suburbs, and soon Har Sinai would follow. This was one of the last High Holyday services held in the old building. As usual, all the polished oak pews were occupied. Because of the heat the back doors stood open. My father's sermon that night was about the prophet Micah and justice and mercy, and as always when he spoke about prophetic Judaism, he was especially eloquent. There was total silence except for his voice and an occasional obligato of relaxed banter from the blacks sitting on the stone stoops of their nearby houses. At one point I happened to glance at my grandmother. She was gazing up at my father with ungrudging admiration.

He was the only person who could make her smile. I never saw her laugh. Mainly she kept to her bed, propped upright by pillows, frowning as she worked on one of her splendid hooked rugs. Whenever she felt well enough to leave her bedroom, she immediately headed for the kitchen. Which is where she and I finally, truly met.

I was a self-absorbed 15 when my grandparents came to live with us, and I resented the intrusion. Superficially, I understood what had happened to them, but my compassion was as perfunctory as my comprehension. I didn't like sharing a bathroom with them. The sight of my grandfather's spare breathing tube lying under its disinfectant solution in a glaring white kidney-shaped bowl made me uneasy. From the time they arrived, I felt myself pursued to every corner of the house by my grandmother's unspoken censure. If I'm drunk and disorderly, I grumbled grandly to myself, what business is it of hers? Who does she think she is looking at me like that, those pursed lips, those disparaging eyes?

Then by chance I walked into the kitchen the first afternoon she cooked in our house. I knew of course it was my grandmother standing at the counter, but for a few seconds I had trouble believing it. The woman authoritatively cracking eggs, separating the whites from the yolks, which she whisked assiduously while adding olive oil drop by judicious drop — this woman was *alive*, eyes glowing. cheeks pink, every movement swift, deft and joyous. She was working all the burners on the stove with the sensitive tyranny of an orchestra conductor. A pinch of salt here, a dab of butter there, a flurry of fragrant spice, nothing measured, hardly anything tasted.

Sedonia, who growled whenever anyone invaded her kitchen, was watching avidly, nodding now and then, expostulating softly. My grandmother took note of my presence but said nothing. I watched for a while, then went away. Dinner that night was fabulous, a marriage of German and Southern cuisines I eventually came to realize was her special trademark.

57

The next time she was in the kitchen, so was I. And the next, and every time I could be when I knew she'd be cooking. There wasn't much talk. Sometimes she'd hand me a beater to lick, coated with cake icings of rich dark chocolate or subtly aromatic citrus. Or she'd nod toward a spoonful of sauce she was holding in an equivocal invitation to sample. In time, after she understood I was really interested in what she was doing, she'd assign me small chores: peeling and chopping vegetables, whipping cream. Occasionally as we were working, our eyes would meet and she'd grant me a tiny, curt inclination of her head. One evening she asked me whether I thought a delicate fish sauce had enough dill. I was ecstatic.

My mother, no slouch in the kitchen herself, seldom appeared while my grandmother was working. I remember once glancing up from potatoes I was intently dicing to see her standing at the end of the pantry, gazing at me. She looked as if she wanted to say something. Instead, after a moment she turned and slipped away, easing the door shut behind her.

My rapport with my grandfather was more quickly and directly achieved than with my grandmother, though not necessarily any more communicative. We began taking walks together. He was one tough old man. Diminutive but compact, he charged along at a sprint, twirling the cane he always carried but never used for support. Even in his late seventies I'm sure he could have outdistanced all the doctors who sentenced him to a life of under-exertion.

We'd stride out toward nearby Greenspring Valley, a luxuriance of honeysuckle and wild rose crowding graceful oaks and willows on the banks of secret streams. Or up meandering Seven Mile Lane and across forested Smith Avenue to the Curtis-Wright Airport—a grand name for a tamped down expanse of scraggly meadow—to watch the stubby little Robins and Wrens buzz through test flights. I'd been reading a spate of French detective stories that designated characters by their initials, so I called him D. He appeared to like the nickname, but it was hard to tell because he rarely spoke.

During the Pimlico racing season, as soon as he'd finished breakfast he'd sit down with the newspaper and pay cursory homage to the news before turning to the Morning Line. Post time for the first race was half past one. By 11:30 he'd have his selections figured out. Promptly at noon he'd grab his cane and hurtle toward the track, three miles away. Weekends when I could, I joined him. D never went inside. He couldn't afford the admission price, let alone the minimum two-dollar bets. Instead we'd mingle with the touts and bookies lining the chain-link fence that paralleled the backstretch. After he'd placed a minutely planned dime bet with the bookie who offered the most favorable odds and lighted a fresh cigar, D would sometimes become chatty. His accent was classic loamy New York—"cherce" for choice—delicately limned with his parents' Manchester speech patterns. He never talked about his own life. Instead he might tell me about Peanuts, one of the horses his family had owned. "Slowest nag ever went to the starting gate," he'd say, his tube whistling as he chuckled. "That Peanuts. Dead last every time. We figured the only way to get a win out of him, we'd start him in the first race, and hope the pack in the second wouldn't catch up to him before his jock schlepped him across the finish line."

* * *

The letters my mother wrote my father to France in 1919 have vanished, but from one of his replies it's evident she had said something like, "I'll help you in your work as much as I can, but don't expect me to change the way I am." And as long as he was alive, she never did. The trouble was, she tried.

She was certainly intelligent, but neither quick nor very articulate. Her curiosity about life's mysteries and anomalies was at best mild and easily diverted. Her apparent complacency drove my father wild. Even during the long period when she was striving to reclaim some vestige of his earlier ardor, she entreated rather than battled. She was only fierce in her loyalties. Once you were her friend, nothing short of grand treason could shake her allegiance. In time, she was to have sad cause for renunciation and disillusionment.

As I grew older and more magnetized by my father, it became increasingly difficult for my mother and me to discuss anything. Yet I always remained aware of her capacity for unfussed compassion. And in early boyhood I was still a direct beneficiary. One afternoon when I was six, just as I was leaving the schoolyard I got hit with a virulent, completely unexpected attack of diarrhea. Liquid shit filled my short pants and began coursing down my naked legs. Mortified, I somehow avoided my schoolmates and propelled my stinking body in the direction of home, zigzagging from cover to cover, flattening myself against trees, wriggling along the foundations of hedges. About a block from my house there was another surge of effluent. I burst through the front door, noisome and blubbering, and froze. My mother was not alone. She and a friend were having tea. Without an instant's hesitation she crossed the room, gathered me in her arms and held me, just long enough to indicate she didn't care how I smelled and looked. She cleaned me up briskly and silently, but I could feel the deep kindness. She tucked me into bed and held my hand, still not speaking, until I fell asleep. I believe now she remained mute partly because she always had trouble with words and didn't know what to say. I also think she was aware that then it didn't matter.

When she married, my mother was a petite, pretty woman of 21, with raven hair and great luminous eyes. However, all the Peyser women tended to plump up in their late twenties, and my mother followed the rule. But despite her ongoing battle against ampleness, she remained a pretty woman, especially when she felt relaxed.

The start of Passover was always one time when the endemic frictions in our household eased. As must already be evident, we weren't what could be called a narrowly observant Jewish family. Emma's rebellion against the dietary laws had turned my father's eating habits eclectic, and neither the Dryer nor Peyser families had recently adhered to *kashrut*. We did, however, ceremonially light the Sabbath candles every Friday evening and afterward blessed the bread and wine. And the Seder was perennially special.

There would be at least a dozen of us crammed around the dining room table. The guests almost always included Father Raymond McGowan and Elisabeth Gilman. Ray, my father's age, lived in Washington and ran the Social Action Department of the National Catholic Welfare Conference. He and my father developed a close friendship while trying to blast away some of the heavier Capitol Hill sediment. A decade after my father's death, McCarthy sympathizers in the Catholic hierarchy booted Ray McGowan out of his job and exiled him to a tiny parish in the Caribbean, where he died an alcoholic. But in the mid-1930s he was young, handsome, voluble, and filled with dynamic hope. Elisabeth was the daughter of Daniel Coit Gilman, Johns Hopkins University's first president. In her sixties then, a spry, homely, brilliant woman, she was the Socialist Party's eternal—and eternally unsuccessful—candidate for Mayor of Baltimore, Governor of Maryland and the U.S. Senate.

My mother knew Ray and Elisabeth were fond of her, and whenever they were around she'd flower. She never tried to participate in the political shoptalk that drumfired around the table during dinner, but whatever she did say was easy and unpretentious, and her laughter warmed everyone. We'd accompany the exuberant narrative of the exodus from Egypt with a lot of sweet Passover wine. Ray and Elisabeth would stumble through their special rendition of *Chad Gadyo*, the melodic Aramaic refrain about the quirky fortunes of a young goat. My father would coax a smile out of my grandmother. Then, for one heartbreaking instant, my father and mother would look at each other as I imagined they might have the day of their wedding.

I suppose my mother had to renege on her promise never to change. My father would have demanded it, maybe not directly or even knowingly, but nonetheless inexorably. The combative road he had chosen was uncertain and lonely, and he needed a savvy confidante. He must have early on launched an impatient campaign to remold her in his own image. She acquiesced, and the result was ruinous.

My mother finished high school a couple of years before she met my father and immediately went to work as a secretary. Her parents couldn't afford to send her to college, but even if they could have, it's doubtful whether she would have gone. She wasn't at all intellectual and in fact was never much of a reader. It took her months to plow through a popular novel. She preferred movies, the schmalzier the better.

A rabbi's wife was expected to be an active member of the Sisterhood, Reform's version of a Women's Auxiliary, and to deliver the occasional paper at discussion groups. My mother agonized for months over hers. She was tenacious about her marriage, but if while she was writing a paper my father had asked for a divorce, I think she'd have promptly agreed. She refused any help from him, though, and if what she finally turned out lacked glitter, it was always straightforward, informative and perfectly organized.

What she loved was gardening; she would happily spend a whole day on her knees weeding. She was a steady golfer, nerveless enough in competition to once reach the semi-finals of the Maryland Women's Championship. But what she cared about most was her home, making sure her family was secure and comfortable.

I don't know which came first, my mother's attempts to change, or Selma. What mattered in the end was that she found herself competing in an arena she should never have entered. To begin with, my mother's fashion sense could be most charitably described as laissez-faire. Selma, on the other hand, was invariably crisply and alluringly turned out. She also seemed to have read everything, and when she talked about what she'd read — or anything else — her throaty, sexy voice could command instant, total attention from everyone in a room. Male *and* female.

61

I find it hard to write about my mother's efforts to transform herself into a dazzling intellectual. The superficial, ill-informed opinions, the painful banality. Then, recognizing the damage she had inflicted on herself — for she was neither stupid nor insensitive — she would take dubious refuge behind a kind of folksy jocularity. "I have to go so bad," she would announce on her way to the bathroom, "my back teeth are floating." Or when someone stifled a yawn, "Oh, am I keeping you up?" The unspoken answer when she was like this was, too sadly, always yes.

My father never put her down in public. Nor as far as I know in private. It might have been better if he had. The alternative was far crueler, the more so because it was probably unintentional. Slowly, almost imperceptibly, he began to exclude her from the core of his life. When he talked at dinner about what he was doing, challenges he was facing, how he hoped to grapple with them, he looked at and spoke to me, not my mother. I knew from the avid way she listened that she had heard none of what he was saying before. I was often upset by this. My defense now is that I was a mid-teenager and didn't know what to do about it. But the shameful truth is, even if I had known, I might not have done it.

My mother got back at my father as best she could. No matter where they went together, she began to be perpetually late. If they were supposed to leave by seven in the evening, my father would start exhorting her to get ready — it seemed to me — in the middle of the afternoon. To no avail. When he could no longer stand watching her interminable preparations, he would stride out to the car and irascibly toot the horn at intervals. She never hurried. It was as if she was saying I *told* you not to try to make me keep up with you. Now you just wait. She would eventually leave the house, looking ever so slightly harrassed but with her head high and a stubborn set to her mouth.

A few years after my father's death, when my mother was 48, she left Baltimore for California. She settled first in San Diego and began working as secretary-receptionist for an optometrist. I took a few months' leave from my U.N. job in Europe and went to California. Among other reasons, I was trying to get my head straight after the failure of my first marriage. But I was already dedicatedly on course toward a new, equally unfortunate, relationship.

My mother tried to rescue me from the impending collision. I didn't listen to her advice, but I did notice how she had changed. She, who had always relied on supplication, now regarded the world aggressively. No one, she told me, was going to take advantage of her. She had also plunged into politics and was now a scrappy worker for the Democratic Party.

We became unexpectedly close. I had never been to California, and she delighted in showing me what was still in those days an entrancing kaleidescope of desert, mountains and sea. We sought out sentimental movies and wept contentedly through a performance of *Carousel* at the Globe Theatre. We ate spicy dinners in honky-tonk Tijuana and remembered my grandfather on excursions to horse or dog races.

Gradually, I began to confide in her. Mostly because I wanted to and now felt I could. But also I kept hoping she would reciprocate, so we could start getting at what really lay between us.

I think she must have sensed I was on the verge of bringing up the subject myself. I knew I wouldn't do it gracefully, that it would doubtless begin with a blurted out, "Look, we have to talk about Dad." The probable awkwardness didn't concern me. What did, and finally ruled out any revealing exchange was her beatification of my father.

She did it obliquely. Little throwaways, not only embroideries of his heroism as a social activist, but also anecdotes implying how harmonious and fulfilling their life together had been.

Not surprising, of course, that she had fashioned and was perpetuating a myth in order to survive. Just as, in a slightly altered context, I myself was doing. Only I didn't know it then.

I wonder what might have happened if we'd had the courage not only to take note of the late emperor's nakedness but to laugh and cry about it a little, and eventually to cast over it some fond, worn, familial garment. But we didn't, and I returned to Europe. The next time I saw her, a couple of years later, my brother Ed was living with her and I had a new wife. My mother and I behaved cordially enough toward each other, but the earlier closeness had ebbed into warm, hazy memory.

And the myth was now codified. A large oil portrait of my father dominated the living room of the house my mother and brother occupied southeast of Los Angeles, in hyper-conservative Orange County. There were also photos, lots of them. And an ever enlarging catalogue of stories— about trips my parents had taken together, things they had said to each other, mutual devotion an implied aura round every recollection. At the time listening to her saddened me. Only very recently have I been able to appreciate fragments of nuance that never entered my consciousness then.

My mother died on New Year's Eve, 1981, in her 84th year. She had been terminally ill with cancer for many months, and long before that her mind had begun to unravel. First her memory slipped away, then her sense of time and place. Toward the end she was completely and continuously disoriented.

Just before Thanksgiving my brother phoned me in Toronto to say he didn't think she had much more time, and I flew to California to say good-bye. It was, I assumed as Ed and I stood beside her bed in the dreary Fullerton hospital, largely a symbolic farewell. She lay gazing up at us without the slightest sign of recognition. The cancer had so emaciated her that her bones jutted alarmingly beneath translucent skin.

It was raining when we left the hospital. We sprinted across to a chrome and formica cafe, garishly festooned for Thanksgiving Day, and chomped on some desiccated turkey and sodden pumpkin pie. My brother and I didn't have many common interests. Our mother's impending death provided a bond, albeit morbid, but we had never talked intimately and we didn't now. I was staying with friends in Los Angeles, so after lunch we shook hands and got into our respective cars.

I sat watching Ed drive away. Then, not really knowing why, I switched off the engine, got out of the car and walked back toward the hospital.

My mother was lying just as we had left her, except her eyes were now closed. A nurse came by to check her IV, glanced at me and left. I was just about to do the same when my mother's eyes suddenly opened and focussed on me. There was such vivid intelligence in them that I recoiled, astounded and maybe a little frightened. She smiled briefly, her fingers rustled against the coverlet, and I understood she was reaching for me. I stepped closer and picked up her hand. Her lips began to move. She was trying to tell me something. Desperately, but no sound came out. I don't know how long we stared into each other's eyes. Then the glaze returned to hers, and the restless pressure of her fingers slackened.

My mother had a sweet voice. She loved to sing, especially sentimental ballads. One of her favorites was "Till We Meet Again", which was popular the year she and my father married. She sang it a lot, gardening, doing household chores.

> Smile the while
> You kiss me sad adieu.
> When the clouds roll by,
> I'll come to you.
> Then the skies will seem more blue...

She also sang to her parrot, an evil-tempered beast who tried to shred any finger poked through the bars of his cage unless it belonged to my mother. He adored her, and while the rest of us blanched, she'd take the bird out of his cage, bring him close to her face, and he'd gently caress her cheek with the side of his bill.

The parrot learned many of the words and a rough approximation of the melody of "Till We Meet Again." In the summer she'd hang his cage on the side veranda, and between random obscenities taught him by clownish guests the parrot would rasp:

Down in lovers' lane, my dearie...

Of all my memories of the house in Baltimore, perhaps the most persistent is of my mother standing beside the parrot in the deep shade of the veranda, everything around them baking and pulsing in the savage Baltimore sunlight. The two of them in tableau, and the bizarre, poignant notes of an eternal duet.

Wedding bells will ring so merrily.
Every tear will be a memory.
So wait and pray each night for me,
Till we meet again.

SIX

I had arranged to meet Lee at 11.30 that morning in the kosher restaurant she and her husband owned on West Pico. There'd been a downpour the night before, the first rain to fall on Southern California in months. When I left the house in Tarzana where I was staying, the sun had already blasted every last drop off the trees and grass, but for once there was no pall of yellow-grey smog hovering over the Ventura Freeway.

I was feeling a little jittery. *Shpilkes*, Lee used to call it. Partly, I knew, it was because I was playing with the time machine again, and I didn't know what might happen when I started pushing the buttons. There was some small comfort in knowing Lee was also nervous. I'd phoned the night before to let her know I'd arrived and to find out when we could get together. "What's wrong with right now?" she asked. I told her I couldn't make it. "I wish you could," she said. "I'm afraid if we don't do it now, I'll back out."

I had last seen Lee in the early fall of 1943. After going together for three years, we had split up the previous spring. It had been a stormy parting. I spent the summer in Baltimore, came back to Cincinnati, passed my Bachelor of Hebrew Letters exam and informed the College authorities that I was dropping out to enlist in the Merchant Marine.

Lee had just got her degree in music. She was a terrific pianist; I always marvelled that anyone so tiny could play with so much power. But concert engagements for 22-year-old novices were scarce, so she was working at the Travellers' Aid booth in Union Station. The day before I returned to Baltimore, I went looking for her. The station was wall-to-wall servicemen, lounging against the wooden benches, sleeping sprawled out on the marble floor, heads pillowed on duffel bags or each other. I wanted to tell Lee what I was doing and why I thought I had to do it. As we talked, some of the bitterness between us dropped away. But despite the tearful Wartime parting, I guess we were both sure that as far as we were concerned, this was it.

Fifteen years later, she wrote me a letter after one of my novels came out. She was living in Arizona then, had married a man named Spielberg and borne him four children. I was glad to hear from her and wrote back, but we didn't keep up the correspondence.

In 1970, I was working on a television series at Universal Studios. My producer was a pale, longhaired young man, extravagantly laid-back even by Southern California standards. One morning he slouched into the office where I was bent over my typewriter and stood eying me for a while with an expression of indolent curiosity. "You might want to take a trip over to the stage," he murmured finally. "Kid director there says you almost married his mother."

Steven was in the middle of a take when I came onto the set, so I had to wait to introduce myself. Which was just as well. It was the first time I'd ever encountered progeny of a woman I'd once been close to. I found the sight of this intense, slightly gawky 24-year-old a little unsettling. I remember, however, being unusually impressed with the way he worked. Most directors of series TV belong to the sausage-making school, their greatest concern being to ensure the links are uniform. Steven was treating this *Marcus Welby* episode as if it were an epic feature, totally oblivious to the deadpan condescension of his jaded production crew.

We had a pleasant talk, mainly about Lee. She was still living in Arizona and had made several successful concert tours. I believe I got her address from Steven, but I never did anything about it.

I turned off the San Diego Freeway at Olympic. A few more minutes and I'd be there. Once again I wondered about the value, or even the advisability, of reconnecting long-severed liaisons. Probably without the troubling epiphanies I'd experienced in Cincinnati, I might have been more reluctant to get in touch with Lee. But I was beginning to realize that the project I'd embarked on was much more complicated than just writing a straightforward biography of my father. I sensed the quest was going to propel me back through even more challenging territory than I'd already encountered. Selfishly, I was looking for help, from someone who'd taken part of the original trip with me. To encourage, protect — dissuade? I didn't know.

I stood on the sidewalk outside The Milky Way, working up nerve to go in. The front door opened. Lee started out, and stopped short when she saw me. We gaped at each other for a few seconds, then laughed and gabbled our way into each other's arms.

The restaurant wasn't yet open for the day. We sat burbling away at a table in a corner of the bar while Lee's young staff stole bemused glances at our septuagenerian reunion. We each covertly assessed what the years had done to the other. In her case the passage had been remarkably gentle.

At one point as we reminisced, Lee's eyes suddenly filled with tears. I remembered how precipitantly her moods could change, bubbly to deep melancholy in an instant.

I told her I'd been back to Cincinnati and had gone to see her house. Her expression clamped shut. "I've never been back," she said tersely. "I'll never go. All I can think of when I remember that house in Cincinnati is how poor we were."

I recalled the shabby carpets and curtains, the flaking linoleum, the sofa whose springs chewed into your bum. The cardboard cartons piled high in every room — dresses, pants, underwear, whatever Lee's father was hoping to flog somewhere, anywhere, soon. But no matter where in the heartland he'd been scratching for a living during the week, without fail he'd return home well before sundown on Friday.

Many times I sat at their Shabbat table. When I recollect those evenings now, along with memories of the candles, the wine goblet and snowy cloth, I do a fantasy switch on Woody Allen's *Annie Hall*. Where Allen was certain Diane Keaton's family saw him as a Chasidic rabbi — long black coat, beard and cornerlocks — I'm convinced Lee's father perceived me as a snub-snouted piglet wearing an Eton jacket. He'd fix his frosty blue eyes on me for minutes on end, saying nothing, just staring. But no matter what he was really thinking, whenever he did finally speak to me, it was always with quiet courtesy. And I'll always remember that when he sang the *b'rochot* over the wine and bread, his voice would often crack with emotion and tears streamed down his cheeks.

Somehow the family had scraped together enough money to buy Lee a piano. It was an old upright, chunks gouged out of its streaky black finish, but it was always kept in perfect tune.

"You want to know what I remember about Baltimore?" Lee was asking. "Well, one day after your father died, we were up on the top floor sorting through some clothes for your mother, and a pair of your girl-friends, two fancy Eastern coeds with their fancy Eastern clothes came up the stairs and I didn't hear them coming and there I was bent over up to my ass in a basket—"She broke off and grinned defiantly. "You know what? I'm rich now. And I'm enjoying it."

Like Randy, she still retained vivid memories of the drive to Baltimore the night my father died. Somehow, there had been a lot of awkwardness and delay in letting me know what had happened—who would tell me, where and how. So by the time I was finally informed, my father's body was in a baggage car en route to Baltimore, and there was no way I could catch that train. The fastest way to get home was to drive through the night. "I'm going to Baltimore," Lee told her mother, who replied indignantly, "You certainly are not," then stood aside as Lee plowed past her out of the house carrying her battered little overnight bag.

A detail of the trip I had forgotten until Lee reminded me. At one point the fog was so dense it was impossible to see the road from behind the steering wheel. Whoever wasn't driving peered out open doors on either side of the car and hollered at the driver if we veered too close to the edge of the macadam. Listening to her talk now about that night, I was moved—as I had been at the moment—by the memory of Lee and Randy saying quietly, simply, "We're coming with you."

For no special reason my mind skipped to spring evenings when I'd walk from the bus stop toward Lee's house. The windows would be open, and I'd imagine that the notes of the Chopin she was playing had crystal-lized and were suspended, still delicately throbbing, against the soft twi-light sky. I'd go into the house, and she'd notice I was there, but she'd keep on playing, and even for a moment after the final passionate note died we'd both stay motionless. Then she'd leap up and run to me.

Lee was watching me now with the small skewed smile I remembered, the one that left her eyes sad. "We were such romantics, weren't we? But then it was such a romantic era."

The restaurant was beginning to fill. Lee called one of the waitresses over and asked her to bring me some chimichangas. Kosher chimichangas?

Bernie, Lee's second husband, had been a successful engineer before he decided to devote his life to Chasidic Judaism. Lee had of course been raised traditionally, but over the years she had allowed her upbringing to blur. Still, when Bernie became stringently observant, so did she.

They decided to dedicate The Milky Way to showing that, contrary to stereotype, strictly kosher meals can also taste good. They hired a Mexican cook and taught him the principles of *kashrut*. The chef brought in members of his family to fill the remaining kitchen positions, gave them a crash course in Jewish dietary laws, and the enterprise was off to an exuberant start. No doubt a number of the Hollywood elite first showed up because the restaurant was owned by Steven Spielberg's mother. But judging by my chimichangas, I figured at least some of them came back because of the food.

"Funny," Lee was saying, "I can't remember how we broke up. I mean, I remember the misery and how confused we both were, but the details, well, they're just gone."

They were for me, too. We began trying to recall, probing for moments and motives with a kind of wry detachment. The green hills of Cincinnati's Eden Park came back, and Lee's white raincoat, and both of us screaming at each other, then crying.

I could feel myself getting more and more uncomfortable.

"I guess," Lee said, "we'd reached the point where we either had to get married or split up."

"Yes," I said, and was relieved when a flock of customers arrived all at once and she had to go help cope with the congestion.

I was thinking about what Dr. Marcus had told me. The girl my father had left, to begin an ardent courtship of his classmate's sister, only to turn his back on her and launch his passionate pursuit of my mother. And then.

I watched Lee work the room, laughing, exuding vitality, skittering from table to table like a cheerful waterbug. I wondered how it might have gone if we *had* married. For one thing, I suddenly realized, there would have been no ET, and for a while I contemplated that awesome possibility. A bearded man entered the bar and glanced at Lee, then toward me. I was aware of cool, speculative eyes behind gold-rimmed glasses. Lee hurried over and introduced me to her husband.

Bernie, she told me later, was adamant in his own beliefs and observances, but he never tried to inflict them on others. She herself followed the ritual requirements out of respect for Bernie, never because he compelled her to. He was, she said, completely open-minded and tolerant.

Maybe, I reflected silently, how exceptional if it's true. Religions abounding in extremes of fervor and proscription are rarely forbearing. I thought about the Chasidic Jews of Israel, hurling abuse and rocks at anyone who dared drive a vehicle on the Sabbath, and insisting on the outlawing of *traif* foods throughout a land whose theological legitimacy they denied in the first place. I thought about the pathological hostility of Muslim fundamentalists toward all non-believers. Or the pious certainty of some Christians that God has personally instructed them to chastise any woman who chooses to terminate a pregnancy.

My father was also a zealous advocate for what he believed. However, he fought with equal commitment to protect the rights of those who disagreed with him. But then, no fundamentalist ever admitted that my father might be religious.

Lee was talking about him now, recalling his warmth and charm one day when he took us to Washington. And something else — an edge of power was how she described it. Lee had never seen Washington, so we spent the afternoon on a round of standard sights — the Smithsonian, the House and Senate, various other government buildings. Lee remembered my father entertaining us with a flood of anecdotes about backstage Washington. "I don't think I felt," she mused, "that he was name-dropping or anything like that. It was just that he'd been involved and he was fascinated and he thought we'd be, too."

We were having dinner that night with Dave Niles. He and my father had a meeting scheduled first, so Lee and I were sent off on a short guided tour of the White House. (By that time, after all my circuits, I believe I knew the spiel as well as the guide.) "I remember," Lee said, "that all of a sudden that day I got some idea how it must feel being the son of a man like that, living in the shadow. But it wasn't till years later, when Steven got to be known the way he is — sure, I'm older, I'm his mother not his child, but I could finally understand, people like that, powerful achievers, no matter who you are, what you become, in a way you always go on living in their shadow."

The night my grief finally tore loose, and she held me while I cried. "I think," she said, "what got through to me while that was happening was not only how much you loved him, but how much influence he had on you."

I told Lee I was going to see my brother. "Oh, Junie," she said. Everyone called Ed Junie, not even Junior, until he was well into his thirties, when my second wife made a firm and justifiable fuss about the childish name. "Trouble," Lee said. "Trouble and everybody's indulgent permissiveness."

I felt myself start to bristle. But only reflexively and just for a moment.

Because about the days when she knew Ed, Lee was right. And I had done my share to make him the way he was.

* * *

My mother wanted her second child to be a girl. I don't know what my father wanted — quite possibly not another child at all. Hardly the coziest atmosphere for a boy to be born into, and it didn't improve. My mother dressed Ed in frilly clothes and alternated between overlooking and encouraging his excesses. Ed lied, stole and threw tantrums. My father either punished or ignored him; there seemed to be no middle ground.

All the while Ed and I were young, I followed my father's lead. I was a better student, an athlete, and being nearly four years older, I was considerably bigger. I bullied him abominably.

Ed became eligible for the draft about a year after my father died. My mother was desperate to keep him out of the Army and appealed to Dave Niles to arrange a deferment. Dave gently but adamantly refused. Ed was inducted and sent first to Europe, later to Okinawa. He wasn't a combat soldier, but not because he avoided it. Like most servicemen, he did what he was told, reasonably well.

After the War he did one of the only two things he never should have done; he returned to Baltimore, ostensibly to complete his education. My mother was by then living in California, so Ed stayed with family friends.

Things didn't go well. He barely held on in school, mainly because he became obsessively occupied with organizing a football team dedicated to my father's memory. He importuned Har Sinai congregants for funds, bought expensive uniforms and plunged into debt.

My mother, in a panic over the havoc Ed was provoking in Baltimore, yanked him across the continent and settled him in beside her. His second fateful move, which could have been entitled Out of the Fire, Into the Frying Pan. I doubt either of them realized how much she was overprotecting him. The more feckless Ed became, the more she rationalized.

She inherited a substantial amount of money and National Distillers stock from the widow of her Uncle Sol and promptly sank it all into a neighborhood supermarket with Ed as her partner. Neither knew even the basic principles of food retailing, but they sailed into the enterprise with such ebullient hopes that it was devastating to watch it slide into insolvency. It was also exasperating, because she never for a moment admitted any lapse in judgment, and Ed went along with the fiction of bad luck all too willingly. Mother defended him furiously. She was able to detect criticism while it was still a speck on the horizon, and she invariably jumped in with a preemptive strike. Especially if she anticipated an attack from me. "All very well for you to lay blame," she'd fume before I even opened my mouth. "Ed didn't have the advantages you had. If anyone had given him just a quarter of what you had handed to you on a silver platter, you'd see where he'd be by now. But he has nothing and it's not his fault and you have everything, absolutely everything!"

Today I understand what she was railing about. Text, subtext and footnotes are legible and touching. But then I didn't feel the gods were exactly tossing big generous grins in my direction. I saw myself as a neophyte writer scrabbling with intermittent success up the glossy Hollywood wall, one marriage shattered, the second unsteady and beset with uneasy dalliances I knew I should have avoided. My mother's diatribes did not leave me kindly disposed toward my brother.

Ed was a good-looking man—tall, wide shoulders, craggy features. Mother deplored the fact that he had no girlfriends. Yet as their years together accrued, they became more and more quasi-connubial. Their friends were mostly married couples, some my mother's age, others closer to Ed's. They went everywhere together: dinners, community functions, holiday trips. Mother would get pleasurably flustered when strangers would remark on how handsome and youthful-looking her husband was. Once, Ed became seriously interested in a young widow. Mother professed delight, then gradually but relentlessly sabotaged the relationship, which in any case hadn't progressed all that far. To this moment I don't believe she realized what she was doing. Nor the terrible loneliness—and the dread of more in the offing—that made her do it.

It's miraculous that with all the pernicious currents swirling around him, Ed was able to achieve any kind of stability, emotional or otherwise. But somehow—by no means perfectly and no doubt at the cost of some pain—he managed to stake out a territorial patch he could call his own. He got a job with the Post Office, and evenings after delivering mail he taught himself the basics of tax accounting. Eventually he built a modest consulting practice, and rented an office away from the house he shared with Mother. He retained his near-compulsive enthusiasm for sports and became competent enough at coaching football to land a part-time staff job at a local high school.

However, he still relied heavily on Mother, and as they both got older, any possibility of Ed's declaring complete independence grew more remote. So I wondered how her death would affect him, whether he would implode, run wild, or simply shrivel away. None of the above occurred. I'm sure he missed her; deprivation rarely notes a distinction between symbiosis and love. But I sensed even during our infrequent and generally perfunctory phone chats his feeling of relief. He seemed to be getting on with his life.

I hung back for quite a while before asking Ed if he'd talk with me about our father. We'd never made more than a few glancing references to him in our conversations, and then usually as a coda to one of Mother's rose-covered figments. I knew we'd be tiptoeing through fields filled with mines, inevitably we'd detonate at least one, and either or both of us could be wounded. Given our history, odds were on Ed as the more exposed.

Finally I phoned and told him what I was trying to do. I said we'd almost certainly get onto some uncomfortable subjects, and if he did agree to help me, he could call a halt to our sessions at any time.

He said he had no problem with our meeting and then casually tossed off the news that he was planning to adopt a son. Juan was 16, a Chicano who had survived a turbulent childhood with his biological family and a succession of foster homes. Ed had taken him in about six months before. He and Juan got on well, and after conferring with Juan's case worker, Ed decided to start the adoption process.

Off the top, I thought this was a terrible idea. Not that I was a first-hand expert on teenagers, but I did have an idea of how self-centered they could be. And unconcernedly cruel. Add to that Juan's history, with its potential of emotional disturbance, and Ed could be begging for trouble. But I said nothing. Even if we had been close, I might have felt it wasn't my business to interfere, and God knows we weren't close.

I guess it was just our lack of intimacy I was thinking about when I checked into the hotel in Anaheim, a block away from Ed's house. He didn't have room to put me up, and I realized I was just as happy where I was. A mouse-throw from Disneyland, I told Gloria on the phone, not feeling as smartass as I sounded.

That night, I took Ed and Juan to dinner in one of those unfalteringly bouncy surf 'n' turfers so many Californians appear to cherish. Juan turned out to look like a huge puppy that was still growing into its paws. Ed boasted about his prowess as a defensive tackle, and Juan put him down with a blithe, unbarbed rejoinder. He and I got into a hot discussion about the Gulf War. Juan's arguments were bright and well-reasoned. I liked the unbelligerent but definite way he defended his convictions.

After a while I stopped talking and just listened to Ed and Juan kid back and forth. Sure, the relationship could turn into a disaster. Either Ed or Juan—or both—could be badly hurt. But hadn't I spent almost my entire life arduously learning that you can never really care for anyone else until you allow yourself to become vulnerable? Even now I still sometimes manage to dance away from putting my feelings on the line. And here was my brother, just going ahead and doing it.

* * *

The next morning, Ed got to my hotel room half an hour late. He was obviously nervous, heading for the bathroom the moment he arrived, and again a few minutes later. I told him once more that he was completely free to stop our talk any time he wanted, including before we even started. I tried not to make what I was saying sound like Jewish Mama Black-mail—look how far I've come just to talk to you, but don't worry about it, I'll be okay. He said no, he really wanted to do this, and I had the feeling he really did, but he was scared. An emotion I could empathize with, and I told him so. We grinned wanly at each other. Okay, I said, why don't we start with your most vivid memory of Dad?

"Well," Ed began, then stopped. We both shifted around uncomfortably. Ed cleared his throat and went on. "I was maybe 11 or 12, and Dad asked me to go on this trip. I don't know why. He never had before, and he never did again. But he was supposed to give a talk in New Haven, and he said we could spend the afternoon and evening before in New York. We took the B & O up. You remember how the Pennsy ran right into New York, and on the B & O you had to change to a bus in Newark, and then that went onto a ferry. But Dad always said he liked it better, he liked the view you got of New York from the river. So did I. Then when we got there, we went to Radio City, Madison Square Garden, Lindy's, places like that."

"What did you talk about?"

"I don't know that we talked about anything much."

"But you were alone together, what—about three days."

"Well, on the train he was always either reading or making notes."

"And in New York?"

"In New York," Ed said evenly, "he was like a tour guide."

I looked at him, thinking of trips I had taken with the same man, and didn't know what to say. Ed saved me the trouble. Suddenly, out poured a torrent of appalling reminiscence, delivered in a soft, almost wistful voice, about how Dad had "mauled" him for this and "belted" him for that. Mauled and belted? I remembered getting strapped on a very few occasions when I'd been particularly obnoxious, and I knew Ed had received more corporal punishment than I. But I had no idea it was anything like the way he was describing it. Even if he's only imagining it, I was thinking, especially if he's imagining it.

"I guess," Ed was saying with a kind of rueful pride, "I inherited my temper from Dad."

Then his mood changed, and he was laughing about an incident that occurred while Dave Niles was staying with us in Maine. We may have been the only city visitors on the lake. We were certainly the only Democrats in the county. Nobody had to ask how the locals felt about Franklin Roosevelt; in Maine it was de rigeur to spit whenever you heard his name.

The closest phone was located about a mile from our cottage, in the general store. One afternoon the proprietor appeared, asking for Dave. "Lady on the phone," he announced. "Wants you to come right away." He paused, the effort of being polite turning his face the color of brick. "Says it's that Roosevelt fella."

I recalled driving Dave to the store that afternoon. There were maybe half a dozen men slouching in tilted-back chairs, feet up on barrels of nails. The receiver of the crank phone dangled, looking as if it had been contemptuuously discarded. The men watched Dave silently, without expression, across heaps of hatchets, rubber boots and calico. The only way one knew they were alive was their concerted reptilian blink every time Dave said, "Right, Mr. President."

And almost guiltily, now that Ed had recounted his New York experience, I remembered another time in Maine. My father did most of his reading and writing late at night or early in the morning, often straight through, one to the other. I would seldom enter his study in our house in Baltimore when I knew he was working. Maine was another matter. Most importantly, there was no study in the cottage we rented. But my father always brought along 40 or 50 books and as many bundles of periodicals as he could stuff into the car, between and around suitcases. A number of the books were pre-publication copies. He would read them all and select several to review on his weekly radio show over WBAL.

He did his "vacation" reading in the cottage living room. Sometimes I'd wake up, and when I'd see a light I'd get out of bed and take whatever book I was currently reading into the living room. I remember how the smell of cigarette smoke and stale coffee mingled with the scent of pine wafting in through the open window.

My father would nod and go on reading. Usually I'd open my own book, but sometimes I'd pick up a volume from one of the stacks on the floor. It might be a new novel, or biography or political history. If the first few pages grabbed me, I'd ask if I could keep it till I finished. When I had, he'd always ask what I thought. He'd listen, then tell me how the book affected him, and we'd go on from there.

Ed was watching me. I realized we hadn't said anything for a while. Okay, I thought, I guess it has to be now. I glanced out the window, then made myself turn back to him before I asked, "How much did you know about Selma?"

He looked blank. Oh God, I thought, uncomfortable and bemused that I was. "I'm sorry, Ed. I thought you probably heard Mother and Dad arguing at night, I thought you knew." I told him.

He didn't say anything for a moment. Then, "I guess I heard the arguments, but I didn't understand what they were about. I guess I thought married people sometimes argued." He paused. "I mean, they laughed together a lot, too."

They did. I knew they did. I heard them.

"Mother never said anything to you about it?"

He shook his head. "To you?" I shook my head. Simultaneously, we smiled and shrugged. "I guess," Ed said after a few seconds, very slowly, "I guess I did know. Something."

"We were both pretty young while all this was going on. You were still very young when he died."

"Yes," he said. "Sixteen."

* * *

At lunch we tried to talk about other things. It wasn't easy. I was interested in sports, and he in politics, but it was as if we were speaking sharply varied dialects of the same language. We just never quite connected. I also writhed every time he addressed a waitress as "sweetheart", and I was conscious of a bumptious awkwardness that surfaced now and then. I knew well enough where he'd got it because I'd also inherited it, and I didn't like it in myself, either.

We had stopped making small talk. Ed fidgeted, then asked, "Did the congregation know about Dad and Selma?"

I told him I thought so, that probably almost all of them knew toward the end, and some might have been aware for a longer time.

"What I don't understand," Ed said, "what I can't figure at all is how five or six hundred families, a lot of them with kids, could sit there week after week and listen to him with such respect and attention if all the while they knew what he was doing."

I told him I couldn't figure it, either, but maybe in a few weeks, after I'd visited Baltimore, I'd have some answers. I didn't tell Ed what Dr. Marcus had told me about the affair with Roberta Gordon. I guess I was still wrestling with that one.

"Unless," Ed was saying, pursuing his own line of thought, "unless he was just such a powerful person, the way he towered over everybody, all the tremendous things he was doing, that nobody wanted to bring him down."

I had to admit, he'd certainly thrown the conundrum into clear relief.

* * *

Back in the hotel room I asked, "Were there any times you felt really close to Dad?"

It was difficult to watch his face while he was thinking, but he was looking straight at me, so I made myself meet his gaze.

"When I was 12," he said after a while, "I had my tonsils out. Some reason I couldn't before that, I forget what. Well, you know how Mom hated anything to do with blood and hospitals, and I guess she was making kind of a fuss about the doctor cutting me with a knife. Anyhow, Dad ended up taking me to the hospital. He was with me, holding onto my hand when they put me to sleep, and the first thing I saw when I woke up was his face. He told me not to try to talk. After a while he gave me some ice cream, and he sat there talking to me. No, I don't remember what he said."

"What made you think I'd want to know?"

"Because it's just the kind of question you always ask. Always did."

We laughed. Another pause, this one almost companionable.

"The time I really felt close to Dad, maybe the only time I thought he cared about anything I had to say, was while I was in his confirmation class."

Confirmation at Har Sinai took place toward the end of May. It was a very special occasion for my father. There were usually a dozen or so young people in the class; their average age was 15. Every Sunday morning they met with my father for three hours. For the first half of the year he'd encourage them to do the talking, in particular to express their doubts and antipathies—about God, religious worship, Jewish tradition. He wouldn't let them get away with platitudes. He made them dig for what they really thought. But he never allowed them to despair or get too confused. He kept the discussion going, and at the end of each session he'd leave them with an intellectual cliffhanger, something that stirred up such lively contention they could hardly wait for the next class. Toward the end of the year he'd draw together all the disparate elements, using the class's most perplexing doubts as a springboard into his sense of the Jewish faith. He related history to belief, and of course made sure they understood the Jewish concepts of justice and social responsibility. And, yes, the moral law. At the conclusion of a simple and moving service in the sanctuary, he blessed the confirmants individually, and to each he added a whispered confidential message.

"We'd drive home after the Sunday class," Ed said, "and we'd talk more about what went on there, and one day all of a sudden I thought maybe I could talk to him about, you know, personal things. And I did, and he asked me questions like he really cared, and..." Ed stopped and sat looking at his hands. "That lasted till summer. Then you came back from school and we went up for our month in Maine, and it was you and him again."

"You must have hated my guts."

"I admired you."

"Ed..."

"Okay, I admired you and I hated your guts. I used to watch the two of you go off fishing, and finally I said to myself, well, I don't really like fishing that much, anyhow."

"I'm sorry, Ed."

He shrugged. "It wasn't your fault. And it's not like I was left alone. Mom was there."

"Did you have the feeling then that I was Dad's son and you were Mom's?"

Ed smiled. There were times when he had a beautiful smile, open and warm. "Well, as long as I had somebody."

We began talking about the night our father died. I told him how I'd called a family friend in Baltimore and asked him to go over to the house and break the news to Mother, and to tell her I was on my way east. I asked Ed how he learned about it.

"I was out somewhere," he said, "and when I came home there was a whole bunch of cars outside and a lot of people in the living room. They didn't see me, and I went upstairs and Mom was in the bedroom crying. I asked her what was wrong and she wouldn't say anything for a while, and I kept asking and then she said, 'Oh Junie, Dad's real sick." Then she started crying again and I went back downstairs and I walked over to one of the men in the living room and I said, 'Is my father going to die?' And he looked at me kind of funny and said, 'Your father's dead.'"

The next morning Ed went with Dave Lampe, the friend I had phoned, to the B & O station. The train carrying our father's body was due in at six, so it was still dark when they reached Carlin's Circle, a major intersection overlooked by a tacky, immensely popular amusement park. "I heard the newsboys yelling and I rolled down the car window. They were waving papers and calling out Extra! Extra! Rabbi Israel dead!"

In my cursory exploration of the Archives material, I had seen the press coverage of our father's death. Until then, I had remembered a huge front page banner, something roughly equivalent to the Pearl Harbor news a couple of months later. Well, the story in the Morning Sun, which would have been the first to carry it, was front page all right, but not a banner. I doubted there had ever been an extra, and even if there had been, newsboys wouldn't have been out hawking it before dawn. Okay, I wondered, why am I niggling, this was part of Ed's personal myth, his version of my rampant hero of the Hunger March. Or our mother's revisionist tales of marital bliss. I had a twinge. Was it wrong to jostle the dead?

"I remember the body was in the dining room," Ed was saying. "The table pushed to one end and the coffin up against the back windows. I couldn't make myself go in and look at him."

Again, my own recollection. The two a.m. silence. Him lying there, a shell so neatly pastelled. The desperate need to talk to him. Hear his voice. Just one more time.

"How did you feel then?" I asked Ed. "Do you remember?"

"I remember. The main thing I thought—I'm not afraid any more. The fear was gone."

I looked at him. I knew I had taken it as far as I should. Maybe farther. But I couldn't keep myself from asking, "If you had to sum up, what would be your bottom line about Dad?"

"He was a great man. He did a lot of good. He fought for minorities, he was always trying to get more for the underprivileged, the underdog." Ed went on like this for several minutes, his speech pattern, even his vocabulary, resonating oddly back to his mid-teens. "And I keep thinking," he was saying, "if he had lived, how different the world might be."

"That's the public man," I said. "There was a private man that you and I knew intimately. Only from what we've been saying today, we knew two different persons. Your private man, what's the bottom line on him?"

"I keep thinking," Ed said slowly, "if he had lived, how different *I* might be."

* * *

I went over to see where Ed lived, one of a couple hundred near-identical units in a development park. It was comfortably cluttered. I recognized a lot of the furniture and sports trophies from the days when Ed and Mother shared a house. There was still the oil portrait of our father, and the photos, and on the wall a framed letter from Roosevelt.

We watched Juan and a friend feed flies to Juan's iguana, a present from Ed. Then Ed and I went downstairs, sat in front of the TV and looked at *60 Minutes* without paying a great deal of attention.

We said little. Neither of us was eager to take the day further. Part of it was emotional exhaustion. But also, once again we had nothing much to talk about.

After a while I said goodbye to Juan and thanked Ed. We exchanged a few cordially neutral phrases at the door. I went back to the hotel, ordered a sandwich, phoned Gloria, then watched movies till I got sleepy.

My father, Rabbi Edward L. Israel, taken in the mid-1930s.

Amelia Dryer Israel, my mother. The photo is also from the mid-30s, taken by my father at the annual dinner of his congregation, Har Sinai, in Baltimore.

My father, mother and me, probably around 1922, in Evansville, Indiana.

Cincinnati, Ohio. My father's father, Charles Israel, holding me. The building in the background is the Dryer Hotel, owned by my mother's mother, who became a legend for setting the most lavish table in the city.

My brother, Edward Junior, late 1930s.

The summer cottage we rented on a lake in central Maine. When my father and I brought in a catch like this, we'd fry some for dinner on the woodstove, and my mother would pickle the rest, using one of her mother's recipes. I'm wearing the sweater I earned for freshman track at the U. of North Carolina. I believe I wore it constantly, until it finally rotted off me.

My mother, father, brother and me outside our house in Baltimore, late 1930s. One of my mother's luxuriant rose arbors is visible in the background.

My father took this of me during the time I worked as a copy boy for the *Baltimore Sun*. The ratty trenchcoat was derigueur for my concept of myself as a newspaperman.

SEVEN

In early April, soon after I met with my brother, Gloria and I drove to Baltimore. I wanted to talk with as many people as I could who remembered my father, though this would now chiefly mean members of my own generation. I had also arranged access to the files in the Baltimore Sun library.

In addition, I wanted to learn more about what took place during my father's last couple of years at Har Sinai. The stormy time.

As I recalled it, until 1939 the congregational scene was relatively tranquil. By then my father and Selma must have been a hot item for at least a decade, but no one cried havoc. Not officially, at any rate. In view of the nature of the community, this was at the very least extraordinary. Baltimore was something of a southern hothouse in which species existed side by side but rarely cross-pollinated. The blacks, comprising about a third of the population, were compacted into a couple of square miles northwest of the harbor, centering around a squalid thoroughfare called Pennsylvania Avenue. The Jews were also emphatically, though certainly more comfortably, ghettoized. Up till fairly recent times, Jews were prohibited by carelessly veiled caveat from settling in affluent gentile neighborhoods like Roland Park. Even today, human rights rhetoric notwithstanding, Baltimore's swank Wasp country clubs admit only a few token Jews to membership.

Given the confined environment and a propensity for smalltown gossip, it's unlikely that a rabbi could carry on an affair with one of his parishioners unobserved, and it's downright bizarre that no one blew the whistle. As I've mentioned, though, my father had a powerful coterie of admirers who could circle the wagons

Among these devotees was a bald, genial salesman in his mid-thirties. Gerald's pudginess and the texture of his skin gave him an uncanny resemblance to today's Pilsbury Doughboy. His wife Naomi, compulsively garrulous and precariously high-strung, vented much of her apprehensiveness on their only child, Arnold, a bright, somewhat klutzy boy. One Sunday in 1937, when Arnold was a member of the Har Sinai confirmation class, my father asked him to take a photo of the group. Arnold clambered onto a folding chair, snapped the picture, teetered crazily for an instant, then tumbled. As he fell, the back of the chair drove upward into his midriff, causing extensive internal injuries.

Complications developed. Arnold drifted into a coma and required massive transfusions. I remember how ashen my father looked when he and I trudged into the hospital to give Arnold blood. He blamed himself for the mishap, and indeed he probably never should have allowed someone so awkward to climb anything more than a millimeter high.

Arnold died. My father mourned as intensely as the boy's parents. Their shared grief appeared to strengthen the tie between our families. Gerald and Naomi were forever at our house, murmuring in the living room with my father, walking distractedly in the garden with my mother. They visited us in Maine for a week the next summer, and gradually their anguish seemed to abate. In fact, the couple was a walking time bomb.

By 1939, the congregation had become so large that my father found it difficult to handle all his pastoral obligations. True, he had once again spread himself thin across an ever-enlarging spectrum of political activity, but the congregation had also decidedly outgrown the capabilities of one minister.

For a while my father tried to gallop off in all directions at once, but after a couple of serious cardiac warnings he resolved to ask his board to give him an assistant. They agreed, but took back the $2000 they had restored to his salary only a few months earlier.

At first, Jonah worked part-time at Har Sinai. Officially he was still director of the Hillel Foundation at a nearby university, and he commuted to Baltimore a day or two a week. He was clever and ingratiating. The congregation took to him, and so did my parents. He relieved my father of a spate of burdensome tasks, and my father allowed him generous access to the pulpit—a privilege not often accorded inexperienced assistants by senior rabbis.

Soon the board confirmed Jonah as permanent assistant. And soon after that the brawl got under way.

It began with a subdued ferment of rumor. I was in Cincinnati most of the year and only caught sporadic hints of the escalation. However, when I came home for the December break, I noticed a vague chilliness between my father and Jonah. When I asked my father what was going on, he uncharacteristically shrugged and changed the subject.

Sometime between then and my next visit at Passover, the lid blew off. At least a dozen of my father's most loyal friends turned against him. Fiercely, vocally. Couples accustomed to dropping in at all hours, sauntering like close relatives into our house without knocking, now shunned our whole family.

Gossip churned the long, narrow corridor that contained Baltimore's Jewish community—from the dark, genteelly mouldering mansions of downtown Eutaw Place northward to the chic, new-minted suburban houses in Pikesville. And two of my father's most vociferous badmouthers were Gerald and Naomi. My father, according to them now, was depraved and unscrupulous, not fit even to sit in the same synagogue with respectable Jews, let alone be a rabbi. And he had murdered Arnold through his willful negligence. Much of the community recoiled from this scattershot frenzy, but many others listened. A congregational crisis appeared inevitable.

I am biased of course, but I believe Jonah encouraged the furor. He was an exceptionally able man. He has since enjoyed a lengthy, distinguished career in the rabbinate. When he came to Baltimore, he was young, probably idealistic. He perceived a situation that may very well have scandalized him. My father was vulnerable. Culpable is a better word. I feel, though, that Jonah exploited his own outrage.

Certainly my father thought Jonah was after his job. He mentioned this to me tersely, without elaborating. We both knew that if there was a confrontation, he would have no defense. Maybe he even wanted the crunch to come.

In any case, he was remarkably non-committal. Especially compared to my mother. All her dormant adrenaline buttons had been pushed at once, and she lighted up like a berserk juke box. She refused to speak to Jonah, but whenever he preached she would sit in the congregation, chin pugnaciously outthrust toward the pulpit, while she fixed him with a baleful, unwavering stare. If she met other erstwhile friends in public, she would treat them to a brisk one-two of hurt and fury before turning dramatically away. My mind boggles now when I consider the Byzantine gyrations she must have put herself through during that time. Maybe she sensed that my father, who would take a bulldog grip on most social issues, had no intention of fighting this particular personal battle. And if he were forced out of the rabbinate, she could in turn be ousted from her marriage. On the other hand, defending my father represented more than a tacit acceptance of his relationship with Selma. In the end, though, I don't believe she ever totted up any elaborate quid pro quo. Her sense of loyalty had been massively assaulted. So there she stood, at the barricades.

The conflict continued to build. A faction in the congregation, spearheaded by some of my father's onetime close friends, was now noisily demanding his dismissal. Gerald and Naomi had become public witches' brewers, synthesizing newts' eyes and dogs' tongues on demand. They should have got what they wanted. From any perspective — logic, mores, professional ethics — my father's position was untenable.

Astonishingly, Gerald and Naomi's cauldron turned out to contain more bubble than trouble. The majority of my father's friends remained steadfast. A number of them were tough, smart combatants in the business world — lawyers, advertising executives, manufacturers. Without being substantially represented on the board, they still somehow devised a successful damage control campaign. The tumult and the shouting began to die. No Captains or Kings departed, and a truce seemed to prevail. My father and Jonah maintained a correct, icy association. The cycle of sabbaths and holy days proceeded; an outsider might not have even been aware that an unsavory little civil war had barely been averted.

Meanwhile, my father's public profile became higher and more familiar to an increasing number of Jews and non-Jews across the country. In June of 1941 he was offered the leadership of the Union of American Hebrew Congregations, an unquestioned honor.

Jonah allowed his name to be put forward as my father's successor. At a special meeting the congregation rejected him by a 3-1 majority and hired Abraham Shusterman, an affable, energetic man who stayed on for nearly half a century.

My father never told me how his defenders kept him from being cashiered. It's possible he never knew. Driving with Gloria to Baltimore that warm April afternoon, I was hoping I might be able to find out just what his friends had to do to save him. And why they did it.

* * *

I hadn't lived in Baltimore since the middle of the War, and before now I'd only returned once, briefly, in 1977. I was researching a docudrama I was writing for Universal and had to spend a couple of days at Johns Hopkins Hospital, so I reserved a room at a downtown Holiday Inn. It was a November afternoon and already getting dark as the taxi took me from the airport toward the heart of the city. Naturally, I didn't expect everything to look the way it had when I left, but I wasn't prepared for what I saw. It wasn't so much that the old landmarks had vanished, rather that someone had started to tear them down, lost interest midway through the job and left them to decay.

Nor was it just the physical deterioration. I found myself comparing it with Munich, which I first saw shortly after the end of the War. Ninety percent of the Bavarian city had suffered bomb damage. Even the major thoroughfares were still choked with rubble. People lived in warrens burrowed beneath the heaps of pulverized stone, and when you walked among them you inhaled the olfactory lingua franca: piss and cabbage soup and shit. That first winter the Muencheners were defeated and despised, hungry and cold. Yet you could feel the perverse vigor in that dreadful city, a will to live. Driving into Baltimore that afternoon, I sensed that behind the gaunt facades lay only more bleakness. This city looked brain-dead. Or in a malignant sleep.

I checked into the hotel, phoned a boyhood friend and arranged to meet him and his wife for dinner. But I couldn't shake off my depression. I thought a walk might help.

Bad idea. The first large intersection I came to, Howard and Lexington, had been when I was growing up the site of three of the city's most elegant department stores. The buildings still stood, gloomy and lifeless, windows boarded, ornamental stonework streaked with grime and crusted bird droppings. Hundreds of gulls, pigeons and crows circled overhead in the darkness, flapping and shrilling.

Disturbed, I fled up Lexington toward the market. My mother used to come here to buy food twice every week, Tuesday and Friday like clockwork. I remember toddling after her through the vast labyrinth of outdoor stalls, delighted by the mounds of oysters, crabs and fish, the fragrant and colorful produce, even the vaguely ominous whole carcasses of animals. When it rained, the stall owners stretched tarpaulins to protect their wares, but not their customers.

Now the market was roofed and walled. The interior felt confined, the vendors seemed listless. Then I spied a stall where they were selling oysters fresh from the shucker's knife. Eagerly, I ordered a dozen and let the first slide off its shell into my mouth, tilting my head back to catch the juices. Disappointed, I tried a second, a third. No help. They just didn't taste the way they used to.

Of course they don't, I chided myself, nothing ever does.

But I felt bereft. I really didn't want to explore further.

* * *

Today was different. We were rolling through the hills north of the city. Dazzling sunlight and an exuberance of new greenery alone might have sufficed to kick-start the spirits. But I was creating a high of my own. For absolutely no logical reason, I felt I was on the brink of learning something extremely important about my father. Here, very soon, in Baltimore. Also, I was looking forward to showing Gloria some of the shards and crannies of my childhood. And maybe, in viewing them now through her eyes as well as mine, to picking up a few fresh insights.

Then too, I didn't expect Baltimore to be as much of a downer as on my last visit. Formidable rebahilitation was supposed to be underway in the city core. The waterfront, already renovated, was touted as spectacular.

I got my first taste of change sooner than I anticipated, on the beltway slicing through what had been woods, rabbits and silence in my time. I zipped past the turnoff I should have taken, and we found ourselves beginning a slow traverse of East Baltimore's cramped byways.

We meandered past endless repetitions of the famous white stone stoops and inched through sets of traffic signals intent on setting world's records for staying red. The sluggish pace made us aware of the heat, which felt more like late June than the first week of April. But not, happily, like July and August, when temperature and humidity teamed up round the clock to make you feel as if you were drowning on top of a barbecue grill. It was oppressive enough, though, and now I found myself noticing that most of the stoops, far from being white, were really a nasty brindle. And we seemed to be running an excrutiatingly long gamut of anonymous, graffiti-bedecked relics. The native's return, it appeared, was not to be so upbeat after all.

Then suddenly, everywhere, scaffolding blossomed. Clinging to the walls of half-restored buildings, bridging the mouths of dank-looking alleys. Dusty stacks of brick, monstrous earth movers, tar drums, everything chaotic but alive. Even though it was Sunday, there was a perception of something happening, in transition.

I began to recognize locales from the past, unbelievably intact, and pretty much as I recalled them. The Gayety Burlesque. The day we first swaggered through its doors as 13-year-olds, into a mouldy, overheated cavern, rows of skewed seats thinly upholstered with greasy velour, where we instantly subsided, squirming self-consciously while a flabby stripper wearily rotated her tits in our direction.

And buildings I remembered which, equally unbelievably. no longer existed at all. "There!" I cried excitedly. "Miller Brothers, I mean it used to be, it isn't any more, how could they have torn that down? The greatest seafood restaurant in the world, my father used to take me there, ceiling fans and cool marble floors, black waiters cool as the marble, you'd swear they knew everything about you and they probably did, they sure heard enough juicy Baltimore gossip, but they never said a word even when you spoke to them, just nodded and kept bringing the fantastic crabcakes and beer."

We were cruising up Charles Street. "And there! That little place, we used to cram in on Saturday nights, cheek by jowl but the smoke so thick we could hardly see each other and there was this black singer and she'd wait till the beer started to tie our tongues in knots and then she'd make us sing along with her. *Sally, Sally, sittin' in the shoeshine shop*, I sang. *When she shines she sits all day and when she sits she shines all day...*

I saw Gloria smile to herself and suddenly realized how long I must have been babbling. She grabbed my hand, and we both started to laugh.

We were staying at a small hotel on Calvert. It was dark when we came out on our way to dinner, but heat was still pulsating up from the pavement. We were heading for a seafood restaurant on Eastern Avenue and decided to drive past the harbor on the way.

It had been tarted up, no question, glitzy malls shooting off in all directions, a giant aquarium nearby and Federal Hill rising clear in the night sky across an iridescent expanse of water. And surely an improvement on ancient memory. Once early in 1944 my ship was tied up for a week very close, I guessed, to where a water taxi was now easing toward a slip. I was on day watch, so I slept at home. Every morning before dawn I'd ride a streetcar nearly to the end of Light Street. I'd show my pass at the dock-yard gate, then negotiate the murky alleyways between crumbling warehouses where rats scurried ceaselessly, not quite beyond sight. On the wharf I'd pause, just outside the glare of calcium lights and look up at the shadowed rustbucket that in a matter of days would be taking me and a fewscore shipmates and a load of munitions out on some chilly grey waters, toward some destination, destiny, who knew? I'd usually stay there for a moment, on the cusp of my identities. Then I'd step into the light, climb the gangway, and midway up I'd change from the intellectual son of a Baltimore rabbi to the fucking oiler ready to fucking go below and stand my fucking watch.

Somewhere from along this stretch of waterfront an Old Bay Line passenger ship used to sail every evening at six for Norfolk, at the ocean end of the Chesapeake. Occasionally when my father had to speak in Virginia, he'd take the boat instead of the train, and sometimes in the summer I'd go with him. We'd share a tiny stateroom, and as soon as we stowed our bags we'd hurry out on deck to sit in the muggy, coppery dusk, listen to the thud of the engines and watch the mouth of the Patapsco recede as the ship moved out onto the broad waters of the Bay.

We ate dinner in the capacious dining room, crystal chandeliers, delicate china, silver cutlery, bevies of whitejacketed waiters racing to bring oysters, crabcakes, cornbread and fried chicken, a real downhome number. Sometimes I think it can't be true, nothing was ever like that, it's another retrospective embroidery, but no, the images are too clear, too indelible.

If there was moonlight we'd sit on the top deck and peer toward the spectral contours of the Eastern Shore. We wouldn't talk much, and we'd usually go to bed early. In the morning we'd be at the rail while our ship was docking. Usually they'd already be handling cargo in berths on either side. I remember smells of coffee, spices and creosote. We'd always stand for a few minutes listening to the squeal of the winches and the black stevedores joshing as they worked or unexpectedly loosing a gleaming arpeggio of song. Then my father would fling his arm around my shoulder, and we'd trundle off to our eggs and sugar-cured ham, biscuits and grits.

It was still uncomfortably warm when Gloria and I got to the restaurant. All around us people were hammering away with wooden mallets, cracking the shells of the succulent little Maryland crabs. We debated, then decided on crabcakes, which Gloria had never tasted. My wife has been writing about food for a quarter of a century. I always enjoy being with her when she tries something new, especially when she finds she likes it. "They're good," I admitted now, watching her expression, then added severely, "but I have to tell you, they don't taste anything like they used to."

* * *

I phoned Virginia, the daughter of one my father's most devoted supporters. She told me she'd arranged for a few old friends to get together with me and talk about my father. Virginia was my brother's age. Back in the days when we knew each other, she was the little sister of my friend Lloyd, now long dead. We could see each other's houses across nearly a mile of fields bisected by the paddock of Tyson's Riding Academy.

Virginia's mother, Mildred, was a good-looking woman with fine, thin features, a disconcertingly direct stare and a frightening reservoir of energy. She was one of a special breed of Jewish women that flourished in those times. American-born, often of immigrant parents, they were dynamic and manipulative, but rarely offensive. Their vitality was their charm. They made anyone they were trying to enlist in a cause feel as alive as they, and therefore flattered. They chaired committees, headed drives, they seldom stopped moving. Their husbands, perhaps of necessity, were silent men, almost always good providers and usually ill at ease in social gatherings. I recall them mainly generically, shifting from foot to foot, smiling indulgently at the bravura performances of their wives.

Mildred and my mother were close. They enjoyed gossiping over cups of tea. Most often, though, it was Mildred who did the talking. She spoke in fusillades which she delivered with a total absence of facial expression and no perceptible pause for breath. Mildred couldn't be called a conventional gossip, for whatever she said behind peoples' backs she'd just as readily address to their faces. Fast and deadpan. What she and my mother had most in common was their uncompromising allegiance to anyone they cared for. When my father came under attack, Mildred's loyalty never wavered.

One of the brighter moments of my brief 1977 return to Baltimore had been a dinner with Mildred. She was then in her early eighties, as lively and compulsive a talker as ever. And as deadpan. "I have a boyfriend," she told me. "Nice man, but kind of stick-in-the-mud, I have to keep him moving. He wants to marry me. I keep telling him no. As long as we're courting, he'll take me out to places. The minute we get married, all we'll do is sit in front of the TV."

The conversation didn't get around to my father until we'd nearly finished dinner. As soon as Mildred mentioned his name, tears began streaming down her cheeks. But she wanted to keep talking about him and she did. She was disappointed that the new Har Sinai library had been named after Abe Shusterman, my father's successor. Not inappropriately, considering Abe's many years of devoted service to the congregation, and Mildred spoke warmly of him. But not the way she talked about my father.

In 1977 I hadn't even begun to formulate the questions that were so important to me now. I wish I had, and I wish I'd been able to talk about them with Mildred.

Virginia's manner on the phone reminded me of her mother. Nowhere near as overwhelming, but I could still hear Mildred's head-on directness. Our get-together, she informed me, was set for the day after tomorrow, in the afternoon. Which would give me a full day in the Sun library, with enough time left over for Gloria and me to do some exploring.

* * *

Our first stop wasn't promising. There was no Temple at the corner of Bolton and Wilson. The ground where it had stood was now a parkette: cement walks among worn patches of grass, a scattering of benches beneath a few forlorn trees.

I tried to describe the old grey stone edifice to Gloria. The exterior had been austere as a fortress. Steps the width of the building mounted steeply toward a gloomy colonnaded recess containing three precisely placed entrance doors. But inside, the sanctuary radiated warmth and a sense of intimacy—light filtering gently through the stained glass windows, the Perpetual Lamp burning above a simply designed Ark. Two white marble wall tablets with gold lettering flanked the altar. One read, in Hebrew and English, *Hear O Israel, the Lord our God, the Lord is one*, and the other instructed the congregants to love their neighbors as themselves.

I remembered the afternoon of my father's funeral, every seat filled, the coffin lying in front of the altar, just below the pulpit. I in his office back of the sanctuary before the service began, leaning against his desk and chain-puffing cigarettes, until someone made me quit because smoke was starting to foul the auditorium.

We were back in the car, driving up Eutaw Place. Oddly, for the moment I was no longer thinking about the old Temple, or searching out half-remembered childhood sites along the way. Instead I was mulling over some of Gloria's memories, stories she'd told me while we were looking around the part of Toronto where she'd lived as a child. Now it was predominantly Greek, but once it had been a lower middle class, Protestant bastion. "A respectable neighborhood," the residents termed it. Gloria showed me her house, her school, the shop where she bought satin-textured candies called wishbones, and finally the church her parents belonged to. Every week she was sent to afternoon Sunday School class in the basement, a nickel for the collection plate clutched in her hand. When she was nine, she decided she didn't believe what she was being taught. She was particularly dismayed by her teacher, a black-clad woman named, really, Mrs. Godsell. From then on, every Sunday she would leave her house, but instead of going to church she'd wander around the streets until it was time to return home. Only she didn't know what to do with her nickel. Obviously she couldn't put it in the collection plate. Nor did she feel she could spend it. So each week she threw it away, into a snowbank or down a sewer.

A couple of summers later, in the middle of the War, she was with her family at their cottage on a Muskoka lake. One afternoon a neighbor came to visit. Gloria remembers her mother sitting in a green wicker rocking chair on the screened-in veranda. As it inevitably did, conversation got around to the War. "One big mistake we made," the neighbor said. "We should have let Hitler finish what he started with the Jews." Gloria's mother smiled and nodded agreement as she continued to rock. Gloria fled and threw up. She has no idea what made her, at the age of eleven, react so violently. So far as she recalls, not one person in her family felt differently from her mother.

And I was wondering, driving the streets of my own childhood, how we know—or fathom—what to accept and reject from our parents. And about the consequences when we fail to disavow what we should.

I took Gloria through Druid Hill Park, which was apparently not yet one of the city's urban renewal priorities. A brackish smell drifted off the reservoir, ripening in the unseasonable heat. The Mansion House, once a regal architectural jewel, looked as if it had begun pleading for a coat of paint at least ten years ago. A shabby sign announced that the Mansion now contained offices for the Zoo, which from a distance appeared as mingy as everything else.

I suppose I could have found all this as depressing as my 1977 visit. But there was that irrational yet increasingly powerful conviction that I was on the verge of some significant enlightenment about my father. Familiar terrain, however seedy it may have become, now only heightened the expectation.

We emerged from the park onto Carlin's Circle, where my brother believed he heard newsboys crying my father's death in the darkness. The gaudy arch through which we entered the amusement complex was gone. So were the roller coaster and the long row of other stomach-churning rides, replaced by a cluster of sober-looking apartment buildings. Off to the right, on a table of land above the entrance arch, there had once been an indoor skating rink. Summers toward the end of the 30s, a lot of name big bands took to the road, and many of them came to Baltimore. Every April the Carlin's management would turn off the refrigerant under the floor and silence the p.a. that had played The Blue Danube incessantly through the winter. Then Jimmy Lunceford would arrive, and the Dorsey Brothers, first ensemble and later with separate bands. On a couple of gigs, Tommy brought Sinatra along. It didn't matter to us that the unbaffled acoustics endowed his voice with a few extra quavers. Entwined couples packed themselves around the bandstand, eyes closed, swaying ever so gently as the boss's silken trombone underlined the ever so melancholy words of "I'll Never Smile Again".

Up Park Heights Avenue now, past the ruins of the Avalon Theater. Once this was the hub of the Russian Jewish community, then as inflexibly cordoned off from the German Jews further north as both were from the Negroes. Now the whole area was almost exclusively populated by blacks, already entrenched past Pimlico and determinedly moving north.

We drove alongside the racetrack, past the chainlink fence where my grandfather and I hung out with the bookies, searching among the geometry of new, raw boulevards for the house where Selma once lived.

Venerable, great-limbed oaks and maples shaded the street. My dominant memory of the house and its deep front porch is that it was cool and peaceful. I wouldn't even try to count the number of times I rode past on my bike when I was fifteen, craning my neck, hoping the front door would open and she'd come out.

Not Selma; it was her daughter Marge I was after. Though I'm sure the bearded Viennese sage could even have wrung a few Oedipal overtones out of that.

Marge was exquisite. Selma's features were broad, striking, always in play, the kind of motion Toulouse-Lautrec captured in his vivid freeze-frames. Marge's face looked like an idealized ivory carving of her mother's. She was warmly intelligent, she laughed a lot, and under the convoluted terms of our family juxtapositions we were like brother and sister. Only I didn't want to be her brother.

I went to summer camp in the Adirondacks that year and wrote her unremittingly lovesick, florid letters. I saw her face everywhere — mirrored on the surface of the lake, floating above the baseball diamond, in the campfire smoke. She was just as mushy as I, but her romance-object then was my tentmate Sonny, who had a prodigious Adam's apple and was very muscular and very funny. All that summer I bombarded Marge with my fevered missives. Hers came back, all addressed to Sonny.

My father knew how crazy I was about Marge. I'm sure now he and Selma must have discussed it, sympathetically I like to think, and probably with an appreciation of the situation's wry potential. But I wouldn't talk to him about it, no matter how much I was hurting. And I was in a lot of pain.

It passed, but it took nearly a year, forever at that age, and gradually Marge and I reverted to being quasi-siblings. More like twins, since only two weeks separated our birthdates. We both went to the University of North Carolina, mainly because of my father's friendship with the president, Frank Graham, an indomitable and charismatic New Dealer who later became a U.S. Senator.

In those days only male students spent the entire undergraduate span at Chapel Hill. Females had to put in acouple of years at the Women's College, fifty miles away in Greensboro, before they were allowed to transfer.

Marge's older sister, Elaine, drove us to North Carolina. Marge was not very happy. Several months before, abruptly and inexplicably, she had blown up like a blimp. Her graceful figure vanished beneath a layering of fat. Her lovely features coarsened.

My lack of sensitivity during the drive down might have been unconsciously vengeful. Mainly I think it was that I was just coming up on seventeen, and I could hardly hold in my excitement, anticipating the days ahead. I wasn't even thinking about how Marge felt, let alone trying to understand how devastated and frightened she must have been.

We pulled up in front of my dormitory in Chapel Hill. Marge caught hold of my hand. You'll write, you'll come see me, she begged, often? Yeah sure, I replied, hauling a suitcase out of the trunk with my free hand.

Until then I had been an excrutiatingly shy kid. Much of my self-consciousness came from being minus a couple of upper front teeth, courtesy of a gene replicating itself among the males of my mother's family. I spent a lot of time shamefacedly trying to cover up my goofy, gapped smile.

The shyness didn't disappear when I entered college. But after a few months in Chapel Hill I was getting straight A's, I joined a fraternity, I made the track team. And I discovered the exhilarating world of girls girls girls.

Saturday afternoons six or seven of us, often more, would squeeze into a jalopy and head for Greensboro. For many years afterward those expeditions and the nostalgia they could instantly summon up remained one of my paradigms for happiness. Clattering along the bumpy macadam, the landscape a blur of red dirt, scruffy little poplars and pines the hue of jade against a turquoise sky, bawling dirty limericks that hilarity inevitably splintered mid-verse.

At the Women's College I'd sometimes have a dope (southern for Coke) with Marge before going on to pick up my date. Most often not. For a while I hotly pursued a grey-eyed South Carolina girl named Jessie, who admonished me long and sternly for saying I love you without being absolutely sure I meant it. Betty Jean from Asheville, ebon-haired, long-lashed and treacle-voiced, simultaneously played me and two of my fraternity brothers on an intricate string and broke my heart for two weeks.

One day I received a letter from Marge. I no longer have it, but I can still remember how the hurt and anger leaped off the page. And the kernel: "You were so insecure, you didn't believe you could do anything, it used to make me sad to be around you. Then Mom and your Dad gave you something to go on, something to help you change. You changed all right. You're so conceited now I can't even stand to look at you."

Remorseful, I phoned, and after suitable negotiations we made a date. For a while we went out every couple of weeks. Very soon, though, Marge slimmed as suddenly as she had ballooned, and once more the admirers swarmed like honey bees. Now we'd meet before or after our respective dates, and confide and laugh, and it was easy brother-sister again.

Two years after my father died, the autumn when I was in Baltimore waiting to be called to the maritime training station, Marge and I fell in love. She was on her way to becoming a psychiatric social worker, and in a few weeks would be going back to school. It was a sweet time, the long Maryland fall. We went to movies, read poetry, took leisurely drives and walks through the Greenspring Valley. When I left Cincinnati, the dormitory matron had given me the balance of my year's meat ration coupons.

Instead of turning them over to my mother, one day I squandered them on a gigantic steak. Marge and I took a frying pan and a loaf of bread into a deep glen smelling of leaf mould and mushrooms. We cooked beside a purling brook and tore pieces of bread and bloody beef with our hands and laughed and kissed and talked about how we were going to save the world.

Sometimes we'd have a drink with Selma. I thought about telling her how the night my father died I had wanted to phone and let her know so it wouldn't explode on her when she picked up the morning paper. But I hadn't been able to make the phone call then, and now I didn't know how to bring the subject up.

For reasons I didn't understand at the time, when I left for training station, I turned my back on Marge. And shortly after that, I began plunging toward my first marriage.

During all those warm, gentle weeks together, Marge and I talked about many things. But never, not once, about the relationship between Selma and my father.

* * *

More than a dozen synagogues lined upper Park Heights Avenue now, including the transplanted Har Sinai, which occupied what had once been the grounds of a gentile country club. Otherwise the neighborhood looked a lot as it had fifty years before. Most of the houses were even still painted the colors I remembered, and the red brick apartment buildings appeared eternal. Only the streetcar tracks had disappeared, buses replacing the Number Five Line's clattering Toonervilles.

Returning to youthful venues, I was discovering, could make you believe you'd just swallowed a random melange of Alice's curious Wonderland brews. One minute I'd feel outsized, too big for these claustrophobic streets, maybe a little too defiantly jaded. For me now the emanation of social incest was too emphatic here. I'd outgrown it and I was glad.

However, an instant later, while passing a house where a classmate had lived, another Alice-potion would kick in, and I'd be reliving the innocence of after-school cookies and milk and my shyness in the presence of my friend's mother.

Sometimes the perspectives collided, as when I was searching for the private school where I'd gone to kindergarten. The grey frame house with the gingerbready trim was no more, one of the area's few properties to have vanished. But as Gloria and I drove past the spot where it had stood, the memory came back of a morning when I inadvertently glanced into the eyes of the adolescent daughter of the headmistress. I always sensed something dark and restless about her, though of course at the time I would hardly have put a name to it. She was gazing intently past me, lips a little parted, and she seemed to be having trouble breathing. I wondered what was making her look so strange and turned to see the school's only male teacher standing a few feet away with the same expression on his face. Now I found myself simultaneously recalling what I had observed years ago and experiencing a pang of regret for the purity of the moment when I first glimpsed lust and had no inkling what it was.

Gloria and I sat in the car outside the house on Strathmore Avenue where my family had lived for two or three years before moving a mile north toward Pikesville. Through the trees I could see the dome of the New Har Sinai. Then, when the property still belonged to the Maryland Country Club, I used to mine a rich trove of golf balls from the woods behind our back porch. The house was still the same clumsy admixture of brick, stained wood siding and brown shingled roof. Looking at the windows fronting the street, even now I could conjure up the appearance of every room that lay behind them.

Fragments of a troubling memory began rising. When I was about six, long before the discovery of antibiotics, both my father and I lay danger-ously ill in separate upstairs rooms of this house. He had pneumonia, I diphtheria. I remember my lips being so cracked they bled, the searing agony in my throat, the jagged, scarlet images of fever. Once, my father stood beside me, swaying as he looked down, his face grey and stubbled, his eyes unfocused. My mother in the doorway, imploring him to go back to bed. Her presence, her care, her hands supporting me, holding the tumbler with the bent glass straw. Her urgent whispered conferences with the doctor just outside the door raveling my dreams. All those weeks she nursed us, two helpless males, at least one of us recalcitrant, while still having to deal with my baby brother.

Sitting in front of the house, trying to distill some essence from the recollection, I started calculating. This would have been 1927. Probably at the time of his illness, my father had not yet begun his affair with Selma. But according to Dr. Marcus, he would certainly have been involved at that point with Roberta Gordon. And soon after his recovery, he would commence his impassioned liaison with Selma. After all my mother's solicitude.

But the truth is, of course, that neither affection nor dedication can ever be regarded as guaranteed emotional investments. Unless we give love freely, without hope of return, there can be no return. Or none that will touch us.

Well and good, this pure theoretical physics of love. More pragmatically, my mother devoted herself to my father. Presumably out of love. He appeared to give her back less than he got. Considerably. With no regard for the rules of the game. At times, if not much of the time, my mother must have been angry. Furious. During his battle with pneumonia, when she stood beside him sponging his forehead to help curb the burning fever, did she ever pause, staring down at his closed eyes? Did she ever let the cloth slide out of her hands, back into the basin of water and mouth with her mind if not her lips the alarming, toneless words? *Die then.*

* * *

It would take only a few minutes to reach the house on Shelburne Road where we lived after Strathmore, but I felt I needed some breathing space. So we ricocheted around. I showed Gloria things like my old public school and the Suburban Club, one of the two local Jewish country clubs.

When I lived in Baltimore an edgy demarcation existed between the older German Jewish community and those who arrived later from Eastern Europe. Regardless of their actual geographical origins, the newcomers were all scornfully referred to in German-Jewish nomenclature as "Russian Jews". None would even be considered for membership in the German Suburban Club. As the Russians grew more affluent, they did what the German Jews had done when they were excluded from the gentile clubs: they founded their own. Rabbis customarily received offers of honorary membership from both clubs. Although the majority of his congregants were German Jews, my father opted for Woodholme, the Russian club.

He loved golf and was a powerful if erratic player; he could hit a wood shot well over two hundred yards, but at least half the time the ball ended up hooking wickedly. He was also, on principle, uncomfortable with the idea of belonging to any country club. It's possible that he eased his activist conscience by throwing in his social lot with the underdog class of Jews. I suspect, though, that he really joined the Russian club because his mother would have hated the idea. Cincinnati German Jews were probably even more snobbish than Baltimoreans. My grandmother knew very well that my grandfather had been born in Lithuania. Indeed, reminding Paden of his lowly lineage was a mainstay of her nightly diatribes. But Memel, the port city my grandfather passed through on his way to the States, was at that time a German enclave. So to outsiders Emma would announce, "Oh yes, my husband is a German Jew. From Memel, you know."

I drove down Park Heights and turned left onto Seven Mile Lane. The curving road had marked one edge of the ghetto I knew. To the north and west the few houses dotting open fields had been owned by Jews. South and east of the Lane was more densely settled — rows of solid, utilitarian dwellings with tiny, meticulously maintained front lawns. A "respectable neighborhood", very much like the one Gloria came from, except almost all the families here had been Catholic, with names like Hartlove and Beeler. I went to elementary school with their children, and because there were practically no Jews in the neighborhood, these were the kids I ran with after school.

The Jewish section was heavily built up now. A few of the houses appeared quite grand. But off to the right, the rows of houses where the Catholics had lived looked just as I remembered them.

The dense woods at the corner of Marnat Road and Seven Mile Lane were gone, though. I told Gloria how we used to assemble here with our BB rifles and split up into two teams — armies we called them. We'd sneak among the trees and undergrowth, stalking one another, blasting away at whatever moved. The little BB pellets could raise nasty welts even when your skin was protected by clothing. We regarded every mark as a badge of valor.

Gloria was horrified. "You could have had your eyes shot out. You could have killed each other!" I stared at her. Shamefaced. The freakish time warp again. Never having considered at the moment how stupid we were, never having given it much thought since. I brightened, a fractious ten-year-old. "But we didn't."

Across from the site of the departed woods I saw the little store, empty now but looking as if it had never been altered. It used to be called the Marnat Meat Market and was run by the Cohen family. The store had been our social center. It dispensed the usual staple foodstuffs. But it also offered gumdrops, licorice sticks, gooey Milky Way bars and a concoction we called snowballs: shaved ice packed into small waxed cardboard trays and flavored with your selection from among a dozen bottles of violently colored syrups. On summer nights the air hung motionless outside the store; millers would stun themselves against the streetlight overhanging the corner and spiral slackly down among us. We'd be congregated on the hot pavement in little gender-segregated clusters. Sometimes when we couldn't stand still any longer, we'd circulate slowly in a ragged paseo—a tension of budding breasts and pubescent male hormones hankering to rage.

Mr. Cohen had immigrated from Poland. With his long ungainly arms, shiny bald head and scraggly moustache, he was almost a dead ringer for a comic strip figure of the time called Andy Gump. Almost because Andy's artist never endowed him with the kind of fear and hostility that used to alternate in Mr. Cohen's eyes. Signals that echoed in the shrill Yiddish he and his sour, pallid wife and their lumpy teenage daughter vollied around the store.

Toward me they were at the same time servile because they knew who my father was and contemptuous because I couldn't speak Yiddish. I'd never learned it, nor had my father, other than a few stock phrases; most gentiles in Hollywood today probably know more Yiddish words than we did. None of my mother's family spoke it. Paden surely knew the language as a child, but Emma would have pilloried him if he'd uttered a word.

However, while I couldn't understand what the Cohens were saying, I was well aware what they must be feeling in that neighborhood. Scarcely a week went by without someone calling me a stinking rotten Jewboy, Yid, kike, sheeny, name it and I've had it flung at me. It was the perceived and cliched gauntlet, you accepted the challenge or you fled. I was too scared to flee. And too lonely.

I was about eight the first time I stumbled home from school, tears streaking the caked blood and dirt on my cheeks. My mother let out a few appalled bleats, then choked back the nausea gore always induced in her. For a few fleeting moments she was ready to march out and commit neighborly genocide, first goy spied, first killed. By the time my father came home, however, she had cleaned my wounds and modified her priorities. I must, she announced, be snatched out of that horrible place at once and enrolled in a private school several miles away—where the student body, incidentally, was more than half Jewish. Her rage returned while she was making her case. She began to sputter, then went completely inarticulate.

I remember noticing that my father looked a little surprised. I guess I was, too, understanding somehow that any show of spirit from my mother was rare. He went to her at once, put his arms around her and held her till her fury subsided. Then he said he'd like to speak to me alone and took me upstairs to his study.

He looked at me, put his hand on my shoulder for a moment, asked if my face still hurt. It was okay, I told him. Then began the liturgy accompanying the rite of passage virtually every Jewish boy throughout history must have experienced. It stirred me then, it can still touch me. What happened to you today, my father said, happened to me when I was your age, and to my father. Paden, I said, they hit Paden, too? My father nodded. But he wouldn't hurt anybody, ever, not Paden. I know, my father said with a little half-smile, I wish he would now and then, but that doesn't have much to do with it. Then he explained to me about scapegoats, and why Jews were continually being forced into that role. I didn't understand everything he said, but I remember being incredibly comforted.

If you want, my father said without a pause, I'll arrange first thing in the morning for you to be transferred to Park School, you don't even have to go back to the other place. But you don't have to answer now. Think about it and let me know when you've made up your mind.

He must have seen from my face that I'd already decided. He put his hand on my shoulder again, just for a second. "You'll have to fight back, you know." He spoke so quietly I had trouble hearing him. "You can't just let yourself get beat up." This, I reflect today, from a resolute pacifist nearing the apogee of his commitment to non-violence.

I fought. Sometimes I won, more often I lost. I tried to wash off the battlestains before my mother saw them, but it didn't matter; next week or next day there'd be more. After a while, though, my classmates seemed to tire of baiting and beating me. They came to my house and were polite to my mother, who treated them civilly if somewhat suspiciously. I visited their houses. We played football on a nearby pasture where broken-field running took on a special dimension among rampant cowflop; we overturned outhouses on Halloween; we shot BBs at each other in the woods. And we hung out at the Marnat Meat Market, or as it was more often called, Cohen's Store. My school buddies never said anything in front of me now about the Cohens, but I could guess what they were thinking.

And I still had to fight. No longer with the Beelers or the Hartloves, but whenever anyone new came into the neighborhood, I was like a gunslinger who had to draw again and again. Not because I was the best, just because I was there.

I told Gloria about all this as I eased the car down Marnat. I wanted to see if the last house on the block still looked the same. It did.

When I was nine, a boy named Wilbur used to live there. A couple of Sundays after his family moved in, one of the Hartlove brothers came to my house. Wilbur wanted to fight me. Now. If I didn't want to, Joe would say he couldn't find me. I looked at him without saying anything. We walked together up to Marnat Road.

It was a beautiful sunny afternoon. As soon as we got there, I realized it wasn't just an ordinary fight. Wilbur's father and maybe a dozen men from the neighborhood were gathered on the lawn. Wilbur's father was taking bets. All along both sides of the street people were sitting out on their porches, watching. A lot of them were women, in tall rocking chairs, smiling and rocking. Driving down Marnat all these years after, I remembered again the story Gloria had told me about her mother.

Wilbur's father had carrot-colored hair parted precisely in the middle and slicked back. He grabbed me and his son by our elbows, thrust our faces together and told us to fight fair, he'd give us the word when. Then he shoved us apart. "Go get the sumbitch," Joe Hartlove whispered.

I wish I had. We were an even match physically, and I really got mad when I heard the men all around us yelling for Wilbur to kick the shit out of the Jewboy. I went after him hard, but Wilbur was a lot tougher, and before long he was banging my head against the cement sidewalk. I managed to claw my way out of his grip and up onto my feet. I was groggy, blood was running into both my eyes, and as far as I was concerned, the fight was over. Wilbur felt the same way, I think. But his father grabbed me and booted me back toward Wilbur. Who then went on to give me more of the same.

When it was finally over I could just manage to see Wilbur's father, sun glinting off his orange hair, grinning at me. I backed away, aware of a total silence on the street. "Goddam Wilbur," I said tentatively, looking at his father. Then the tears bubbled up. I started limping back along Marnat toward Seven Mile Lane, sobbing. "Fucking cocksucking bastard Wilbur!" I bellowed. And that was just for mild openers. I staggered between the rows of houses, tears and blood streaming down my face, shrieking every obscenity I'd ever heard, conscious in the intervals between outbursts of people staring from their porches and the dead, heavy stillness.

* * *

When I arrived in Munich during the dreary, brutal winter immediately following the War, I wanted very badly to be able to communicate with the Jews I met, almost all of them concentration camp survivors. But practically none spoke English, and I no Yiddish. However, I knew the chief ingredients of classic Yiddish were Old High German and Hebrew. So when I first went into Jewish DP camps, I would address the natives of Warsaw or Lodz or the *stetls* of Ukraine in a garbled mix of bad Hebrew and worse German. At first they'd just gape. After a moment, inevitably, they'd snicker, then guffaw. I took some satisfaction feeling that this might have been the first time in many years that some of these veterans of Nazi hospitality had really laughed. And eventually I did learn a kind of primitive communication.

I went regularly to Moehlstrasse, a shattered grey street not far from the Peace Angel that served as a rialto for Jewish survivors. All around me there'd be flurries of bargaining, urgent little secretive conferences, a blast of anger, a matching burst of laughter. Energy, a pressing obligation to live. I was constantly aware that only a few months before, nearly everyone here had been starving behind barbed wire. By now I knew something of the price many of them had paid to survive, how painful—and frequently dehumanizing—their choices had been. It only increased my admiration for their courage, their unquenchable stamina. Jews. My brothers.

But were they? What did I really have in common with them? Returning now to the fountainhead of my own acculturation, it suddenly became vital for me to understand. What makes me a Jew?

Certainly not religious observance. I respect the right of anyone to rigidly observe the Sabbath and practice *kashrut*. I have no desire to do so. Since the Holocaust, many Jewish leaders—including a number of Reform rabbis—have urged Jews to pay more attention to their religious tradition. Doing what Jews have done for milennia, they contend, practicing the ancient rituals, praying together, will produce richer inner resources, help us to better withstand adversity. Maybe. But since I can't believe in a personal God, I find formal worship empty. And in many instances hypocritical.

Yet I feel very strongly Jewish. Why?

Perhaps then it's the vulnerability. My humiliation sixty years ago on Marnat Road scarcely bears mention beside what happened a decade later in the Warsaw Ghetto or the shower rooms of Treblinka. But if we learned only one lesson from the Holocaust it was that such insignificant incidents can be microcosmic. Assimilation, as influential German Jews sadly discovered, offers no turnstile deliverance from persecution.

So maybe I'm saying I'm a Jew because I have no other choice. Gloria could take a critical look at her religion, decide it wasn't for her, and walk away from it. Nobody's going to whisper behind hands, "Look at her, trying to hide it, but you can always tell, can't you, plain as the nose on her face, she couldn't be anything else but a Methodist-Presbyterian."

Not that lots of Jews don't think about escaping their origins. And maybe more than ever admit it openly would like to. Not such a hard thing to understand. I mean, who in possession of all his marbles welcomes being a target for every redneck in the world who thinks it's time to kick some Jew butt? Hence maybe the clandestine pleasure when told you don't look Jewish. And the rash of name-changing, to something less Jewish-sounding. Many American Jews received their anglicized names courtesy of Ellis Island immigration officers who couldn't pronounce Szmajzner or the like. But numerous others in succeeding generations made the alterations on their own. Nor is the practice restricted to North America. When a branch of my family migrated in the nineteenth century from Eastern Europe to South Africa, they changed their name from Israel to Isdale.

Yet — and I've thought about this very carefully and tried to be honest — if I were offered a safe-conduct out of Judaism, ancestry obliterated, fresh start under the never-were-a-Jew program and all that, I wouldn't take it.

When my father debated Clarence Darrow in 1930, a segment of his windup argument ran something like this: "It has been alleged here tonight that Judaism is a religion of narrow legalism. Yes, there are Jewish laws, and yes, we respect and uphold them. But that is not all there is to Judaism. Indeed, it was a prophet of my faith who in the most forceful terms rejected blind ceremonialism and formalism. He did not believe ritual alone represented the true worth of the Divine. Nor do I, and that is one reason I remain a Jew."

One reason, and certainly one I can agree with, but that's not the heart of it. I don't think my father felt it was, either.

Okay, what then? For one thing, the history. The knowledge that I'm descended from a people whose recorded past goes back nearly 6000 years. Not an easy bunch, the Jews. Stubborn, rebellious, sometimes avaricious, often wrongheaded. But passionate, too, and capable of instinctive understanding and deep kindness. A people not ashamed to preserve even in early epics a sense of its heroes' frailties.

A people who in the brutish debut of human experience recognized that justice, humility and mercy urgently require one another and made the amalgam a keystone of its credo.

An ironic people, cherishing in its inner lore the most trenchant irony of all: the more you try to eradicate us, the more you ensure the survival of our fittest, and so our adamant and eternal perpetuation.

These are things I can articulate. There's more I can't get to with words, only feel. It's not easy to be a Jew. It may be even harder to explain why you are one.

EIGHT

I could feel Gloria watching me as I looked at the house. Possibly with the same writer's analytical curiosity I had felt observing her outside her family home in Toronto. Knowing some of the events that had taken place behind that stolid brick facade where she passed her childhood, wondering how the things I didn't know had shaped her—enlivening, warping, strengthening, tempering, whatever the mutating equations might dictate. Later, probably, she would ask me questions about this house. For now she was content to sit quietly beside me in the car, allowing me time with my ghosts. What a load of bullshit, I told myself impatiently, it's only a house.

Yes, of course it was. The open side veranda where my mother had sung duets with her parrot was enclosed now. Aside from this there seemed to have been no alterations.

The surroundings, however, had certainly changed. Even up to the time of my father's death the house had stood alone amid fields luxuriant with tall grass and otherwise unobstructed except for a few gnarled wild fruit trees. Now habitation and fastidiously pruned hedges abounded. I no longer had a clear view across to the house where Mildred, Virginia and Lloyd had lived. I guessed the riding academy was long gone. I wondered idly, though, about the mint patch just beyond our back hedge where I used to gather the makings for juleps, whether that had survived. Mint was unbelievably persistent.

One of the distant houses I had been able to see when I lived here belonged to a wealthy criminal defense attorney named Harry Wolf. It was a large red-brick colonial structure fronted by formidable cream-colored columns and expansively flanked by emerald lawns. On the way down Park Heights I had noticed that the property had been taken over by the Baltimore Hebrew Congregation, another of the synagogues resettled from downtown.

During my early teens more Jewish families with sons my age began moving into the neighborhood. Gradually I started hanging out more with them and less with the Hartloves and Beelers. Harry Wolf let us play football on his lawn, which at the very least made a change from dodging cowpats.

There was a story involving the house we lived in. Harry Wolf had once owned the property. During this time Jack Hart, head of a notorious pack of bank robbers that killed frequently and without provocation, was finally apprehended. He retained Wolf to defend him. There wasn't much of a case to be made, but while waiting to be sentenced, Hart escaped and remained on the loose for a couple of months. The house my father eventually bought was empty then, and it was persistently rumored — but never substantiated — that Wolf had allowed Hart to hide out here.

Hart's getaway driver was a feckless young Jew named Walter Socolow. The police picked him up at the same time they collared Hart, and Walter was given life with no possibility of parole. No question, Socolow had been a pretty rotten kid, but after several years behind bars, it became evident that he deeply regretted what he had done, and further, that he would be an excellent candidate for rehabilitation.

My father tried to visit Walter a couple of times a month. Often he took me, and sometimes Marge, along with him. The Maryland State Penitentiary was and still is one of the grimmest, grimiest buildings I've ever seen. At that time, the interior more than lived up to the exterior promise. I remember the succession of corridors all painted a watery green and the carbolic smell not quite masking the reek of feces. The echoes were terrifying. Fragments of male speech, indistinct and ominous, seemed as we turned each corner both to meet and pursue us. And the clangor: keys screeching in locks, metal reverberating against metal. Years later when I wrote police shows for radio, I was always tempted to say to the sound men who were simulating prison noises: no no, you haven't got it right, the hollowness, you're missing the hollow core.

And the hopelessness. Walter was a thin, quiet man with a grey complexion and a tentative, dispirited manner. After five or ten minutes, my father could usually get him to start talking. Nothing very momentous, or very lucid for that matter, a jumble of what he had for breakfast and what he was reading and his job making license plates in the prison machine shop. I never knew what to say to him, and I don't remember that Marge did, either. It didn't seem to matter. At the end he'd be smiling more often, sometimes even at Marge and me.

Over the years my father and others endeavored to have his sentence modified so he'd be eligible for parole. Unsuccessfully. So far as I know, Walter died in prison.

I glanced again at the house, up toward the third floor dormer. My room. One night when I was fourteen, two friends and I took less than half an hour to chug-a-lug a pint of rye in Druid Hill Park. I had never drunk hard liquor before, but I was fine as silk all the way home, giggling on the back platform of the Number Five streetcar and up the dark stairs to my room. Then, inevitably, the moment I lay down I was up again. No time to make it to the bathroom. I puked out the window onto the steep slate roof, so raucously I knew they had to have heard me all the way to Pimlico. I dragged myself back to bed and lay shaking, expecting the worst. I didn't have to wait long. Footsteps on the stairs, the door opening. My father. Feigning sleep, I watched him through slitted eyes. He stood in the doorway for what seemed forever. Then he was gone.

The next evening before dinner he poured himself a glass of rye and casually asked if I'd like one. I was just managing to keep my gorge down, but also wondering my God, how did he know it was rye? I didn't really want to dwell on that. No thanks, I said, I don't think so. Well, my father said, let me know when you'd like to try some, and we'll drink together.

For several years the stain remained on the slate roof below the dormer, defying rain, snow and even the buckets of scalding water I would surreptitiously dump over it. A persistent advertisement for the ingredients of Maryland whiskey.

The room below mine. Could one still detect there — as you're supposed to be able to do at St. Paul's in London — the vestiges of voices past? The quarrels? The laughter. The laughter?

I could have got out of the car, gone up to the front door, told whoever answered my ring who I was and asked if my wife and I could possibly look around the house.

I could have, but I didn't want to. What I had come for—the presence of those who had lived there—was powerful enough from this distance.

* * *

I finished high school at Baltimore City College in February, 1937, graduating midyear because I had skipped some grades along the way. I couldn't start university until fall, so in the interim I worked as a copy boy for the Baltimore Sun.

The A.S. Abell Building at the corner of Baltimore and Charles, which housed the Sunpapers then, was a comfortable, even sloppy kind of workplace. Staircases of worn marble, dim and cluttered walkways, chipped desks and erratic lighting. It also housed a more than adequate share of *Front Page* stereotypes. Reporters tended to slouch exaggeratedly and wear their fedoras shoved back off their foreheads, maybe so you could better observe their cynical expressions. Cigarettes dangled from the corners of their mouths as they typed and strewed ash over their copy. Our boss on the four to midnight shift told everyone he was writing a novel and nipped incessantly from a quart of bourbon he kept in his top drawer. By ten he had usually passed out at his desk, head cradled on his arms, but we all liked him and covered as best we could for the rest of the shift. No one stopped strangers in the building or even cared who they were. Anyone who wanted could walk into the morgue and rummage through the files.

The second morning Gloria and I were in Baltimore, I walked down Calvert to the Sun's new complex of buildings. I had obtained permission to work in the library, as the morgue was now called, but even so I was stopped and interrogated politely at the security desk. The guard gave me a badge but wouldn't let me go upstairs until someone from the library came to escort me.

Another indication of change. The Director of Library Services was a black woman, her assistant white. In old Jim Crow Baltimore. How innocently evil we were in those days gone by. I lived in the house of a man who believed in and campaigned for Negro rights. Yet even he deferred to Jim Crow, as did I. The white schools I went to, the segregated movies and restaurants my father and I patronized.

The assistant brought me a pile of microfiches. Too bad, I thought as I settled at the machine, my father never had a chance to see what had taken place. Obviously, there was still a very long way to go. But in 1941 when he died, with the callous railroading of the young black men in Scottsboro, Alabama of such recent memory and lynchings still rampant in Maryland, how much more disheartening the prospects for change must have seemed.

I switched on the light, adjusted the focus and found myself grinning and shaking my head over the first quote I came to, coverage of a sermon my father delivered in 1926, when he was thirty. "Although there were those during the Dark Ages who called themselves Christians, none of them adhered to the ideals and principles of Christianity. If it hadn't been for the Jews and Arabs, who kept learning and commerce alive, civilization would have had to start anew." Vintage Ed Israel all right, but new wine then, still fizzing a little.

I zipped back and forth across the fiche, wondering idly about my insistent hunch that I was due to find something revealing about my father. I'd had flashes of prescience before. Most—especially the thunderbolts that assured me I was destined to win next week's lottery—came to nothing. Still...

The clippings preserved on the fiches were randomly collated, and there were uneven gaps in the chronology, possibly due to the Sun's onetime relaxed custody over its files. In 1928, my father addressed the National Methodist Episcopal Conference, the first Jew ever to do so. In 1933, the paper devoted three column inches to the details of his being bedridden with grippe. Back again to 1928; churches should be taxed, my father declared. In the same year he defended religion in its ongoing battle with science, but argued that much of the conflict stemmed from "religious leaders in exalted places trying to hold onto power".

I got my job on The Sun through my father. It took him a while to arrange it, in retrospect I'd guess maybe only a couple of weeks, but when you're sixteen eternity sets in quickly. It might have been just adolescent impatience, or possibly a more complicated stroke of rebelliousness, but after about a week of waiting I knocked on my parents' bedroom door early one morning and announced that I had to speak to my father right away.

They slept in twin beds by then. My mother was just getting out of hers. My father was sitting up, a couple of pillows behind his back, surrounded by the kind of dog's breakfast that seemed to accompany him everywhere— in this case the morning paper, a sheaf of 3x5 notecards, a splay of periodicals, a book or two and the everpresent ashtray filled with butts.

"I just wanted to let you know," I said, "since it doesn't look like The

Sun job is coming through, I'm going to look for opportunities elsewhere. Put out some feelers." I actually spoke like that sometimes. It's a wonder anybody listened to me. Even my parents.

My mother smiled. I think she was pleased by what sounded like initiative, my not being content to be handed a job. My father knew me better. Well enough for starters not to rise to the Sun-delay bait.

"And where," he inquired casually, "are you thinking of putting out feelers?"

"The News."

My mother gasped audibly and glanced around the room. Though the term foxhole hadn't yet been coined, I'm sure she was looking for one. But neither my father's expression nor his tone changed. "And why would you want to do that?"

"Why not? It's a newspaper, isn't it?"

"Owned by Hearst."

"So? His money's as good as anybody else's."

My mother set off full steam for the adjoining bathroom. My father lit a fresh cigarette and immediately stubbed it out. That was the only indication I had of any turbulence beneath the composed veneer. It was enough. But I'd come too far to back off. "Let me just give you an idea of a few things Mr. William Randolph Hearst has to answer for," my father said, and began to speak about yellow journalism, Hearst's cynical warmongering during the Spanish-American conflict, his vicious anti-labor policies and his role in the demise of the League of Nations.

I knew he was just warming up. "You don't have to tell me about Hearst," I said.

Even this didn't bring on the blowup. "Well then," he replied, "since you know all about him, if you can honestly tell me that you feel comfortable lending your intelligence and energy and spirit to Mr. Hearst and the things he stands for—all you have to do is tell me that and I'll back your decision all the way. Say the word, and from this second on you'll never hear one word of reproach from me."

A long, long beat. I could see the steel in his eyes. And behind that the kind of hurt that bordered on tenderness.

I sighed. "I'm sorry."

The relief in that room was palpable. "I know," he said, lighting a cigarette and dragging deeply, "how anxious you are to go to work. And I'll tell you something else. I would never recommend you for a job at The Sun, or anywhere else, if I weren't one hundred percent sure you could handle it." Only then did he smile. I think I did, too.

"Wars are not fought any more for democracy or ideals," I was reading that my father had said in 1928, "but for oil, commerce, rubber. It was for these things that the last war was fought." He was denouncing the dispatch of U.S. Marines to Nicaragua, a move for which he blamed banking and mahogany interests. "We were deluded then, but we see the truth now. Our boys were sent to Siberia (to fight the Bolsheviks) because there were loans to the (Czarist) government that American bankers wanted protected...Do not be surprised if at some future time your boys and mine are herded together to a battlefield to defend some banker's investments or somebody's gold."

Nine years later in 1937 he was still opposing war but beginning to waver. He advocated a Constitutional amendment which would take the power to declare war away from Congress and make it dependent on popular referendum. However, he felt constrained at that point to deny he was a pacifist, which he had been for the past dozen or more years. On the one hand he declared that war "would mean the end of democratic government". On the other he was agonizing over the frightening gains Nazism had made and beginning to feel war was "inevitable".

I plunged straight into the riptide of his confusion. I had been working at The Sun for a couple of months when I got the notion that I wanted to go fight for the Loyalists in Spain. I was underage, which meant I'd have to get my parents' permission, but I knew how my father abominated Franco, so I was feeling fairly jaunty when I broached the subject.

My mother made a big to-do, which I had anticipated. It was my father I was watching. Today I suppose I could make a reasonably accurate guess at what was going through his mind, but then I couldn't get a reading. "Well?" I asked.

A barely audible sigh, and a grimace to match. "You're sixteen years old."

"That's why I have to ask permission."

"You're not getting it."

"But I've heard you say that if Franco wins in Spain—"

"No," he said, and I knew that was that.

I was bitterly disappointed. I kept a close watch on wire service reports at the paper and thought a lot about how exciting it would be if I were there, covered with red Spanish dust, lobbing grenades for democracy. Don't talk to me about dictators, I thought subversively, I really understand firsthand what they're all about.

I'm sure that was why I acted the way I did a month later when my great-uncle, Congressman Teddy Peyser, took my father and me to lunch. Uncle Teddy told us he had an exciting surprise. He had spoken to a Maryland Congressman who owed him a favor and it was all set, he just needed me to say I wanted it which he was sure I would, and my father's okay of course. He sat back and gave us a toothy hustings smile. How would I like to be appointed to the United States Naval Academy?

Good old Uncle Teddy. The bon viveur with his silk shirts, Liberty ties and hand-stitched suits, his wide ingenuous grin in his wide florid face. My father was fond of him for being exactly and unapologetically what he was, but at that moment I think he would happily have backhanded him across the restaurant. Uncle Teddy must have had some idea of how my father felt about war and the military. But then his pronouncements had been turning ambivalent of late. Besides, Uncle Teddy the politician understood very well the cosy dichotomy between public proclamation and private interest. "He'd make a fine naval officer, Ed," Uncle Teddy beamed.

"I think—" my father began.

"I think I'd like to think about it," I interjected quickly, and was rewarded by the flash of anger in my father's eyes. But he said nothing, only nodded grimly into Uncle Teddy's sparkling smile.

Given my gap-toothed malocclusion and my astigmatism, I doubt I would ever have got past the Naval Academy's front gate. Even if I had, considering how much—six years later—I detested the boot discipline at the maritime training station, I might never have survived the plebe year at Annapolis. Anyhow, the Naval Academy wasn't what that struggle was all about. Nor did it end when I told Uncle Teddy a few days later thanks, but I'd decided not to take him up on his offer.

I was struck now, even as I started getting bug-eyed from too much microfiche glare, by the breadth of my father's political vision, and by what a durable, against-the-stream battler he was. In 1931, speaking to the Conference of National Religious Leaders on Unemployment and Crime: "We are told that this government does not wish to hear any more appeals for a special session of Congress to do something (about the growing poverty in the nation). What they really want us to do is to appeal for patchwork bandages to cover a festering wound. Any minister who asks his congregation this winter to contribute food and clothes is doing wrong." There's no question, he went on, food and clothing are desperately required. But it's the government that should be providing for this need. And we as religious leaders should be pushing the government to act, instead of allowing them to hide behind our appeals to our congregants for charity. "Any minister who makes such an appeal and does not also make it clear where the responsibility truly lies is derelict in his divine mission."

And in 1935, even as his Zionist conviction intensified, he was still perceptive and courageous enough to voice a sentiment as unpopular in the Jewish community then as it is today. "The Jews must have the right to settle and build the wastelands of Palestine, but they must regard the Arabs as equals, raise their economic and cultural standards and create social and economic bonds."

As the days grew warmer in the spring of 1937, a little vestigial crust of frost lingered between my father and me. I knew it was because of the Naval Academy incident, I figured he was waiting for an apology, and I supposed — since I had done the provoking — that I owed him one. But I didn't want to say I was sorry, because I didn't think I'd been entirely in the wrong. So I crabbed and tacked my way toward penitence without really getting any closer. Then one morning after a midnight to eight shift I was coming up the front walk just as he was leaving the house. I suddenly realized this was the first time in weeks we'd looked each other in the eye, and I didn't want that to go on. "I wasn't serious —" I blurted, "I mean, I never really thought I wanted to go to the Naval Academy."

"I know," he said.

But as was and often is my wont, I couldn't let it lie. "What would you have done if I had gone?"

"Disowned you, what else?" He wasn't smiling.

"Even when I got to be an admiral and could get you Army-Navy tickets on the fifty-yard line?"

"Seems to me," he said evenly, "we already have enough competitive sport right in this house."

We gave each other a quick hug. Then I went off to bed, he to work.

I stayed on the midnight to eight for the rest of the spring, and we started having dinner together downtown a night or two a week. I'd go in the back door of the Temple around seven and climb the short flight of squeaky stairs that led to his office. The anteroom was long and narrow, lined with somber portraits of my father's predecessors. The uncarpeted floor, which creaked as loudly as the stairs, was black with age and ground-in polish. By contrast, my father's study was small and cheerfully lighted, books floor to ceiling on all four walls. He worked behind a massive oak desk, which at least once was a source of embarrassment.

We almost always had a dog, and my father's favorites were toy Boston bulls. He used to take one named Jurgen—after James Branch Cabell's novel—to the office with him nearly every day. Jurgen would lie quietly at my father's feet, concealed from visitors by the frontal partition of the desk. The only problem was that, periodically and unpredictably, Jurgen would turn flatulent and create an instant miasma.

One day an Episcopalian bishop my father had never met arrived for a meeting. Jurgen slept through the exchange of greetings, and my father forgot he was even there until suddenly the air started turning rank. The bishop was stodgy, and for once my father's aplomb deserted him. He tried to ignore Jurgen's emissions, but that soon became impossible. Nor could he manage now to explain. Finally Jurgen ripped off a richly audible blast. My father was horrified, but all he could think to do was look down and call, "Jurgen, stop that!" Once the dog was on this kind of roll, he could go on for hours. So Jurgen kept farting and my father kept glancing down and saying, "Jurgen, stop!" Eventually he gave up, but Jurgen didn't, and the bishop finally made an abrupt departure. The Lord alone knows what he thought about his visit to the rabbi.

Sometimes when I'd come in the evening to pick him up, my father would be reading or writing. He was more apt to be on the phone, for quite a while. I never minded the wait. My father was partial to nineteenth century literature. Among the muddle of Judaica, political philosophy and the latest novels were the complete works of just about every Victorian poet. I first encountered the dark charm of Swinburne and Matthew Arnold during those warm spring evenings in the Temple study. All the windows would be open. In the background there'd be gathering dusk, black voices off the street and my father's genial negotiations on the phone. I'd postpone switching on a lamp as long as possible, so as not to dispel the vividness of love and portentous horizons, lust and death.

As often as not we'd have dinner at Miller Brothers. Occasionally friends would stop by the table on their way in or out of the restaurant; sometimes they'd sit down with us for a few minutes. But mainly we were by ourselves. We rarely, as I remember, discussed anything significant. The Orioles maybe, or what movie we might want to see after dinner. Or he'd tell me stories about his HUC days. Like the one about the self-important professor, freshly arrived from Europe, who became incensed when his students protested that they couldn't understand him. "Weeth da ooksapseen," he spluttered, "ef ee foo vohwaals, Em spahkeng parfack Angleesh!"

Miller's was always packed. Despite the ceiling fans, bodies and brilliant lighting pushed up the temperature. The streets outside, dimly lit and nearly deserted at this hour, felt agreeably cool. We'd walk until it was time for the movie. Afterwards, saying goodnight in front of the theater, I'd sometimes notice how weary my father looked. But I knew that when I went off for my shift he'd head back to his office for a few more hours of work.

I came to the end of the microfiches, flipped off the machine, returned the sheets to their folders and sat back in the chair. Just in that instant I had a clear, acute sense of how much I had missed him. And for how long.

* * *

I spent some time thinking about my meeting with Virginia and the friends she'd invited to reminisce about my father. Gloria suggested and I agreed that it might be better if she didn't come with me to Virginia's. Especially in view of some of the questions I intended to ask.

The trip from downtown to Pikesville used to take at least half an hour. Now, point to point via the Jones Falls Expressway it lasted only minutes. The trade-off for Baltimore, as with any sizable city today, was the concrete spear thrust into its heart.

I crossed Greenspring Avenue onto Old Court Road. Some of the original buildings dating from when this was all farms and forest still existed, but I had to look sharply to locate them. North of here had always been a rigidly delineated white gentile stronghold. Much of it still derived its character from the presence of the Valley Hunt Club and St. Paul's and St. Trinity's schools, but apparently many of the old barriers were disintegrating.

Virginia lived off Old Court Road, less than a mile from the street where she'd spent her childhood. Her husband had died several years before; her children had long since moved out and now had offspring of their own.

I parked in the driveway and she came out to meet me, a spare, attractive woman in her mid-sixties, less brusque in person than on the phone. There was certainly a resemblance to her mother, in looks and manner, but where Mildred came off as impervious, Virginia seemed sensitive and vulnerable. She led me into the house, a sprawling bungalow filled with graceful work she had created during her years as a ceramist.

The three men Virginia had asked to come were waiting. Martin was a couple of years older than I, Herman and Morton a year or so younger. I had known all three since boyhood, but like so many of my other Baltimore ties, these had withered. All of them had been active in Har Sinai; so had their parents, and their parents' parents. All three lived fairly close to the houses in which they'd grown up.

As we small-talked, I felt a little jealous. These four friends, they didn't have to come searching for their roots; they lived in daily touch with them. The envy was momentary. I knew that as surely as they were destined to thrive here, I would have died. Nothing judgmental. Some stay, some have to leave. Still, I had to admit a yearning for continuity and all its subtle permutations.

The five of us grouped around one end of a long refectory table, and I told them about the memoir I was hoping to write. The public man of course, but the private person as well. Especially the private person. Warts and all, I said, and underlined it.

They were happy to talk. It was evident that they recalled my father with affection and respect. "There was something about the way he related to people," Morton said. "To everyone. Children, old people, whoever he was talking to it seemed like he could speak that person's language and understand what they were trying to say even if they weren't saying it."

Herman, I remembered, had been an exuberantly intractable kid. His voice changed early and grew instantly deep and reverberant. He had used it mainly to express rage and protest. "I was terrible," he rumbled now. "I'm talking really bad. God knows what would have happened to me if Uncle Ed—your Dad—hadn't taken me in hand and tamed me. His politics, though, they were something else. Naive. Ridiculous. Way too far to the left."

"You would have called Ghengis Khan left-wing," Martin said. "There's not an inch of space to the right of where you sit." They needled each other a while longer in the amorphous "Bal'mer" drawl I had lost years before but now found myself acquiring again.

"I just remembered something," Martin said. "I believe it happened around 1936, anyhow I know it was summertime and I was very much involved with the Boy Scouts."

"Been a goddam straight-arrow scoutmaster all his life," Herman growled. "Still is, always will be."

"We were having a big camporee," Martin continued, not even glancing at Herman, "Out in Druid Hill Park, we were camped down the hill from the Mansion House, tents, everything. Your father came out just before it got dark, I think he was supposed to make a speech, but before that happened we saw this bunch of men, maybe a couple dozen, marching toward us. They were pretty rough-looking and they were wearing uniforms and carrying flags and banners with swastikas on them. We didn't have to guess who they were, the Nazi Bund, we knew they'd broken up all kinds of meetings and gatherings, especially ones where they knew there'd be Jews. And that was just what they had in mind now, we could see their leader getting them into position to charge into the camp.

"Well, we were just a bunch of kids and pretty scared I guess, and I don't know what would have happened, but then all of a sudden there was your father walking calmly across the grass, straight toward that bunch of Nazi thugs, right up to the leader himself. He started talking. I don't know what your Dad said, but after maybe five minutes the leader just turned and beckoned to the others with him. And then they all walked away, out of the park. And your father came back to us, just like nothing had happened."

The recollections ran down. I was pleased, naturally, to hear them praise my father, but there were riddles I was hoping to solve. I shuffled my notes and prepared to get on with it.

Something happened then that I hadn't counted on. I knew this was the time to bring up the subject of Selma, and all at once I realized there was no way I was going to do it. I made a few lame attempts to come at it obliquely and bombed. So much for the interviewing skills of a professional journalist.

Talk continued, but on more general subjects. I heard, among other things, a colorful description of the 1968 riots, when Baltimore blacks exploded out of their ghetto, trashing everything in sight. Most of the stores in the area were Jewish-owned, and the hostility aroused then between blacks and Jews had never wholly subsided. Riveting, but I wasn't getting my questions answered, worse, I wasn't even asking them.

"I have to go," Herman said after a while. I thanked him, and then the other two were leaving.

Virginia came back from the door. "You didn't get everything you wanted," she began abruptly, sounding like her mother.

"I feel like a jerk," I said.

"When I was saying goodbye to Herman, he said, 'I wasn't going to be the one to tell him.' Why didn't you just ask?"

"I just couldn't," I said.

Virginia looked at me, then nodded. "I don't know if I could have, either. Well," she went on without a break, very Mildred-like. "We'd better go have some dinner."

On our way to the Suburban Club, Virginia told me that yes, she'd known about Selma, and of course she knew that's what I'd been trying to get at earlier, but like Herman, she wasn't going to bring up the subject if I didn't.

"You're making me feel ever so much better," I murmured.

We were coming up to where Old Court Road joined Park Heights. To the right lay Druid Ridge Cemetery. One night when I was thirteen, on the shore of the lake just inside the gate I'd fumbled through my introduction to serious sex, with a girl from Marnat Road. The same street where I'd been pummeled by Wilbur, to the delight of his carrot-top pop. Off to the left was a somewhat smaller pond, the water hole on the Suburban Club golf course. Whenever it froze over, which wasn't often, we'd skate and play hockey there. One night three of us got overeager, went alone to the pond, ventured out onto a black skin of new ice and plunged through. Passage rites fluttering everywhere in the burnished Maryland sunset.

"My mother once told me," Virginia said suddenly, "when she first found out about Selma, she went straight to your mother and told her. And your mother said, 'Well, that may be so, but he sleeps in my bed at night'."

I smiled and sighed, thinking how typical of my mother the story sounded, the awkward bravado, probably delivered with her chin thrust out, hardly able to wait till she could go off alone and weep. Or maybe she cried then, in Mildred's arms. Mildred was peremptory but not cruel. She had undoubtedly gone to my mother as a friend.

"Do you think she went to my father, too?"

"She might have. You know what she was like. If she felt like saying something, she said it."

"Okay," I said. "Here was her rabbi, also her friend, but above all her rabbi. She finds out he's having an affair with a member of the congregation, a married woman, the wife of another parishioner. This was Baltimore, the 1920s. Your mother was part of all that. How could she let my father get away with it? For years? And even defend him publicly?"

Virginia shrugged. "I'm your brother's age, remember? I was still a kid when your father died. Most of what I know I got from my mother. But only much later."

"And she never explained?"

"You knew her. She talked a lot, but she said only exactly what she wanted to say. Never a word more."

We arrived at the Club and sat at a window table. People I knew or thought I knew floated in and out of the room. A few wore golf clothes, most were dressed less casually. Some were children of old friends, looking enough like their parents for me to be able to identify them. It was a strange mosaic, memory and sagging flesh and clear-eyed freshness kaleidescoped, a disconcerting but oddly intriguing warp.

I told Virginia I was trying to locate Selma's daughter. I knew she'd moved away from Baltimore years ago but I didn't know where. Neither did Virginia, she hadn't even heard anything about Marge for a long time, but she'd ask around.

We ordered crabcakes. Delicious. I found it a kind of charming sociological note that I had to come to a Jewish country club to find crabcakes that tasted the way they used to.

Virginia and I talked about what we'd been doing over the past half-century. Then we drifted back onto the subject of our parents. We recalled her father, a moody and laconic man who owned a trucking business where he spent eighteen hours of every day. I told Virginia a story my mother had told me about Mildred. She was driving somewhere and stopped for a traffic light. The second the light turned green, a man in the car behind her started honking impatiently. Mildred very calmly set the handbrake in her car, turned off the engine, got out and slowly walked to the driver's side of the car behind her. She waited for him to roll down the window, then inquired sweetly, "Were you calling me?"

Virginia smiled. A little ruefully, I thought. Mildred must have been something of a mixed blessing to have for a mother.

I drove her back to her house and took down the phone numbers of the three men who had been there that afternoon. Just before we said good-bye, Virginia remarked thoughtfully, "I can't tell you why my mother defended your father, knowing what was going on with him and Selma. I don't know why she didn't go after him for what he was doing, but I do think she was so in love with him she wished it was her."

* * *

Back in the hotel room I phoned Martin and apologized for not having asked earlier in the day what I was going to ask him now. I tried to make it clear why I needed to know. There was a pause after I finished. Then Martin said, very precisely, "Yes, I believe I heard something about Selma.

And you have to remember how young we were then. Whatever I know is what I heard, or overheard, my parents talking about. And the name I heard most wasn't Selma. It was Anna Smolin."

I sat for a moment after hanging up, not knowing what to think. Then I tapped out Herman's number. This time I left Selma's name out of it and just reminded him what he'd said to Virginia when he left her house that afternoon. "Aw, come on," Herman growled, "what do you want to stir all that up for? He was a great guy, tell the good and forget everything else."

I was persistent, and either convinced him or wore him down. Yeah, he said grudgingly, he'd heard talk, also mainly from his parents, and he gave me a name. It wasn't Selma. Nor was it Roberta Gordon, the woman Dr. Marcus had mentioned, nor Anna Smolin.

I was laughing when I came off the phone. "My old man," I said to Gloria. "My God, never mind when did he work, when did he find time to sleep?"

That was because I still didn't believe what I'd heard. Then I did. So much for prescience, I thought. Next time stick to the lottery. Then I couldn't joke any more, because that's when the anger began taking over. I couldn't even contemplate phoning Morton.

Maybe, I thought, maybe I am Biff Loman after all. Even with the Salesman long dead and me in my seventies. But it was much more involved than that, and I knew it.

* * *

Houses of worship often attract extremely suggestible personalities. The charisma of the pulpit can all too easily transform a supplicant into a groupie. And if that's not enough of a sexual weapon, there's always the confessional. Ministers of every faith hear their congregants' most intimate secrets. It's not difficult to exploit the vulnerability of this kind of confidence. Any minister who does is as guilty of malpractice as a carnally manipulative psychiatrist.

My father had to have known all that. He could have left the rabbinate. Yet he chose — or was compelled — to go on as he had. Being a powerful spokesman for social principle, and at the same time abusing the privilege of position. At any rate, that was certainly how it looked.

I was remembering more all the time about my father the man. His warmth and concern, his humor. Now more than ever I was aware of his brilliant activist record and the uncompromising sense of principle he brought to it. I hated the idea that he might in retrospect be compared to some kinky sleazebag evangelist or one of the pathetic priests who fumbled and fondled their way through a darkened children's dormitory.

* * *

Before we left Baltimore I went back, alone this time, to the parkette at the corner of Bolton and Wilson. By now I had learned that when Har Sinai moved out to Park Heights Avenue, the old Temple was sold to a black Baptist congregation. Three years later the building caught fire and burned to the ground.

When I came home in the late spring of 1940, the end of my first year at the College, much of my conversation with my father — and our conflict — was about the War. But one brilliantly sunny morning inside the building that used to stand on this spot, he preached a vibrant sermon using Shelley's "To a Skylark" as a text, weaving the poet's words through references to Jewish moral law. We started home, and as usual he sent the car rocketing around curves in Druid Hill Park. "You know..." he began, then stopped. I turned to him, waiting. He was looking straight ahead. I knew the fact that he was driving had nothing to do with the pause; we'd had some of our most animated conversations to the accompaniment of squealing tires. Finally, he continued. "This morning was the first time since I was ordained that I've ever used the word 'God' in a sermon." He shook his head, and I had the feeling he didn't want to go on with it.

But I also felt that inside this intensely political, enormously complicated animal that was my father, some elusive spiritual transformation was taking place.

The next year I embarked on some laborious theological grappling of my own, and I'd bring my quandaries home to my father. How come, I'd ask him, the theologians know so much about God? How are they able to delineate so precisely just who the Lord is and isn't, how He looks and speaks, what He will and won't do for the human race, and why? How do they *know*? The more I listen and read, I said, the more ridiculous it sounds. All the blathering about The Revealed Word of God. The only word we really have is theirs. And what they preach to us, all these learned authorities, isn't it just a sophisticated way of saying, "For the Bible tells me so"?

My father didn't give me any clear answer. Either he was still formulating his own outlook, or he felt I had to come to mine on my own.

I did. Eventually I came to believe in the mystery and wonder of ineffable forces, the formidable beauty of the universe and the way it's expressed in the intricate balances of our own planet. I'm sure some pattern exists, fashioned by an energy and intelligence none of us has yet remotely begun to comprehend. But this isn't good enough for the theologians of the formal faiths. To survive, they must cut enigma and grandeur down to their size. And like all manipulators, they protect their turf by labeling skepticism ingenuous.

This began to lead me through some pretty cynical territory. How many of those who return again and again to the world's houses of worship, I wondered, do so chiefly in perennial fulfillment of a bargain? Believe and receive. At the very least, be seen to believe, because when everything's totted up who knows, and why take chances? The fear of God?

Yet I have known those who within this intimidating and essentially degrading concept found fulfillment. Lee's father, who believed without question that God was testing the Jews by inflicting misfortune upon them, and that one day He would send the Messiah as He promised, and in this prospect lay eternal joy.

My Uncle Dorman, a cool, pragmatic scientist, who quietly and adamantly believed in a personal God and took pleasure in the opportunity to worship Him.

Father Ray McGowan, who related his dedicated social activism directly to God's bidding. When Ray stayed overnight with us in Baltimore, I shared my room with him. We would sometimes talk half the night, especially after I became a rabbinical student. He would explain to me, simply but fervently, the relationship he tried to maintain with God.

I wish I had this kind of faith. It would be both exhilarating and comforting to be so inspired. In the end, though, you either believe or you don't in an omnipotent God who—albeit inscrutably—has the best interests of humankind at heart. I don't.

But I am perpetually struck with wonder at "what a piece of work a man is". We mortals are such a stew of nobility and greed, grace and fear, vitality and savagery that we inevitably and compulsively brutalize whatever beauty we create. Yet even as we destroy our past, we regenerate hope for what is to come.

In my father's time the world's future appeared dismal. That expectation was nothing compared with our prospects today. Not only have we placed our planet in jeopardy. For the first time in our history we possess the means to obliterate it. I'm not at all sure we shall survive. I am certain we must continue to try.

I know this was how my father felt. For him, man's humanity to man possessed a hallowed meaning. And toward the end of his life he seemed to be struggling toward something else.

'Struggling', I thought as I walked across the ground where the old Temple had stood, might turn out to be a particularly apt word. If faith is indeed a series of involved transactions, what about the bargains my father made? With those who trained him for the rabbinate. With my mother. With his cohorts in social action, with his congregation. With his conscience. Each separate and yet every one inseparable.

Where was it all leading him? Was he beginning to make a bargain with God? With Mephistopheles?

How did my father's faith relate to his breaches of it?

NINE

We detoured to Cincinnati on our way back to Toronto. I wanted to sift through the archival material again and take away copies of whatever looked promising for detailed study. There was an abundance: my father's letters to my mother from France, a handwritten diary from 1930, magazine articles, correspondence, sermons. I was trying to keep up my enthusiasm and energy, but the truth is that by the time I got back to Toronto, I was just about running on filial empty.

I sat at my desk staring at Xeroxes and wondering for the umpteenth time whether I could go on. Whether I should. I'd stopped being angry even before we left Baltimore, but I was still hauling lots of other heavy emotional baggage around. Disappointment. Betrayal. Hurt.

I felt a little silly being so confounded at my age by my father's ancient pecadillos. But that didn't stop me from looking up dictionary definitions of the word womanizer. *One who practices adultery or consorts illicitly with women* came off almost soothingly academic, but Webster's Thesaurus packed a somewhat meaner wallop. *Cassanova, chaser, Don Juan, lady-killer, masher, philanderer.* The period quaintness of the words only made them seem more depressingly apt.

Without the information Dr. Marcus had given me, I might have shrugged off what I'd heard in Baltimore. And I guess until my visit there, I'd been hoping that the legendary Marcus memory might have gone creaky with age. I was convinced now it hadn't.

I wondered how many other episodes there had been, and whether my mother had known about them. And Selma — the woman my father made a point of telling me he loved — when he began with her, was it a case of "forsaking all others", along with the chasing, lady-killing and mashing that went with the territory? From the sound of things, probably not. How much had Selma known?

In May I flew west for the three-week screenwriting workshop I conducted every year at the Banff Centre for the Arts. Whenever I could, I went for long solitary walks among the mountains, trying to get some perspective on what I thought and how I felt. I knew I wasn't exactly one to be passing judgment on my father. The moment I broke up with Lee in 1943, for example, I concentrated on taking the fiancee of one of my best friends to bed. At the same time I was juggling another intense involvement, a callous little Captain's Paradise that soured abruptly with a pregnancy panic. Then the interlude with Marge, followed too quickly by my first marriage, in which I didn't remain monogamous for long. Hardly an admirable record. The fact that each of these relationships possessed for me its own complicated rationale of love — or what I believed to be love — is no excuse.

But reprehensible as I was, I was at least a reprehensible free agent. My father wasn't.

A few days before I left Banff, I trudged and puffed my way up Tunnel Mountain. At the top, I found myself alone on the bare rock ridge. I stood for a long time gazing up the Bow Valley, toward the narrow canyon where the river emerges from the heart of the snow-peaked Rockies. It's the kind of scenery that's traditionally supposed to complement grand decisions. I made a decision then. It was far from grand. Well, I thought, I've come this far. If the rest really gets too tough to take, I can always walk away from it.

When I got back to Toronto, I wrote a letter to my father's long-ago assistant, Jonah: "You will no doubt be surprised to hear from me. Maybe, considering my intemperate behavior when we last met — some 50 years ago if memory serves — you'll be less than pleased. But I hope you won't dismiss out of hand the request I'm about to make."

I told him about the memoir I wanted to write and added, "I'm aware that in your time in Baltimore a certain amount of friction developed between you and Dad. I believe I know some of the reasons why, but neither my memory nor my understanding is complete. I want to know more—I need to know more if I'm to depict my father as accurately as I want to—and you're the only person who can help me." I had no idea how he'd answer, or even if.

About that time I read in The Times of London an interview with the writer Dominick Dunne, a onetime intimate of the Kennedy family. At one point, speaking of the President, Dunne said, "What chances he took with his Mafia mistress." Yes, I thought, and in an altered but still recognizable context, what chances my father took.

The gamble with Selma was understandable, but what about the others? What drove him? Some Kennedy-like appetite for conquest? A preoccupation with jeopardy? Some deeper desperation?

If my mother had the answer, she determinedly took it with her to the grave. I speculated on what Selma might have known. Or even sensed. Maybe, if I ever located Marge, she'd be able to tell me. But I wasn't having much luck tracking her down.

I waded into the archival material, warming up with the typewritten documents. With reason: my father's handwriting made most doctors' prescriptions seem like calligraphy exhibits. Interesting that over the years my brother's writing took on a marked similarity to my father's. In fact, after Ed dropped the word Junior from his name, their signatures looked almost identical.

From scraps of correspondence I learned that my father, early in his student days, had regularly held Saturday morning services at Cincinnati's Jewish Home for the Aged. So had I, and I found it a little surprising that he had never mentioned it. Or maybe he had and I'd forgotten. I doubted that. The experience itself was too enduring. Even now I could see the rows of pale, mottled faces, the clouded eyes. Some of the congregation had tics, others spasms of palsy; many showed tracks of drool at the creased corners of their mouths. But they were all so attentive. Not one pair of eyes left my face throughout the entire service and sermon. It took a couple of months for the message to get through my youthful zeal and vanity, that behind that sea of raptness there was nobody home. No, not true. When they tottered up the aisle and waited patiently to murmur in turn, "Oh rabbi, what a beautiful sermon," gradually you realized that they hadn't understood a single syllable. Many hadn't even heard. But when they clutched your hand and held on, squeezing spasmodically as they strove to speak, and when you talked to them quietly and asked questions, even when they couldn't respond verbally, you knew there was somebody home, all right.

I began deciphering my father's diary, which had been written during the summer of 1930, when he crossed the country delivering a series of lectures and sermons for Jewish Chautauqua. He made the entries mainly aboard trains, which didn't improve their legibility. But it was his first trip to the Far West, and once I got past the worst squiggles, I could feel his excitement. Everything caught his attention, everything fascinated him. The soil color of the Badlands, melancholy Indians mechanically chanting, drumming and dancing for tourists in railroad stations, the splendor of a mountain sunrise. He was 33 then. I had the sense of a very young man who, like Elizabeth Barrett Browning's poet, "hath a child's sight, he sees all new." It was my first real perspective glimpse of my father. I had some feeling now of what it must have been like for other adults to know him then. The spirit, the ebullience, the ingenuous zest, the charm.

And the anger. Conditions in the sordid company mining towns of Utah infuriated him, but he knew this was far from his beat and there was nothing he could do. Instead he vented his frustrated rage against the complacent, hedonistic Jews of Los Angeles. In their luxurious temple he preached a sermon about the rights of workers and the obligation—a Jewish obligation, he emphasized—to pay decent wages and to provide safe and congenial workplaces. Several of the congregation walked out. "I gloried in that!" my wrathful father wrote, also noting that those who remained gave him a warm reception.

Later he added more reflectively, "Religion without the element of social protest means nothing to me. I love the mystical. It is part of my innermost philosophy of life. Yet mysticism run riot is selfishness of the worst sort. A pulpit which preaches only the beauty and sanctity of the God of things as they are rouses my ire, especially in an atmosphere of wealth and affluence. It is such filthy hypocrisy. What? Thanking God for our own prosperity, for our own sense of 'ease in Zion'?"

On this trip he also experienced frequent wistful moments. He fell in love with Santa Barbara, and the diary speaks in a veiled and cautious manner of how pleasant it might be to live there one day with someone very dear to him.

My father had never encountered an overt homosexual advance. He described how a "rather nice-looking and cleancut" young man on the train smiled at him and he returned the smile. In the dining car the man kept smiling at him, then followed him back to his seat and began caressing him and running fingers through his hair. My father was flustered; the young man realized at once he'd made a mistake and retreated. But afterward, my father began thinking about the mutual embarrassment and wondered whether it might be helpful if there were recognized exchanges where homosexuals could gather and pursue relationships more confidently. When he returned to Baltimore he began advocating the idea publicly — to the discomfiture, no doubt, of his middle class congregants in the year 1930.

This prompted a memory of August, 1940, the summer my father and I clashed so fiercely over the War. I was very left-wing, very romantically populist, and after our month in Maine I decided I needed to see the United States. My way. I would hitch rides, sleep under the stars, work where I could. I was nineteen, and my mother raised the requisite protests, probably expecting my father to seal them with his veto.

He didn't. Early one morning he drove me out Reisterstown Road to the city limits, where I intended to start hitching. I was carrying a rolled-up sheepskin coat, a toothbrush and razor along with an extra shirt and pair of shorts in the pockets. My father didn't say much. Whatever apprehensiveness he was feeling he kept to himself. He even understood that on this occasion I didn't want to be hugged. We reached the city limits. He held out his hand, wished me luck and drove away, not hanging around to see if I got a ride.

I did pretty much what I'd said I wanted to do. I slept on the ground, wrapped in my sheepskin, shivering more than I expected. One rainy night in Illinois, a cop saw me huddled under the leaky roof of a park bandstand, took pity on me and let me sleep in an empty cell in the local lockup. I shovelled wheat in Kansas and picked up other bits and pieces of jobs. A lot of the time I was miserably lonely, but I kept that out of the breezy postcards I sent home.

What made me think of the trip now was the recollection of an afternoon in Oklahoma. A farmer stopped his pickup, and I got in. He was blond, blue-eyed, rugged-looking, probably in his late twenties, and he spoke in a quiet, lazy drawl. He was headed for Tulsa, he told me, a hundred miles away. We chatted amiably for a few minutes. Then he turned to me and asked gravely, "Wouldn't want a fella to suck your prick, would you?"

"No," I replied with matching gravity, "thank you very much."

He nodded, pulled over to the side of the road. I got out. He gave me another sedate inclination of his head. I nodded back, and he drove away.

On my first visit to the Archives I had only got the flavor of the letters my father wrote my mother from France. Now, working through them more systematically, I found myself growing involuntarily indignant. My God, I thought, this man was so immature, so juvenile. And in a little over a year he was going to be my *father*!

He *was* immature, he was 22 years old and he was totally, extravagantly in love with my mother. I got an impression of what we today might call laser focus. The white-hot intensity. Nothing, no one else, mattered. I knew that kind of concentration. I'd done what my father had done. I too had meant it. Numerous times. I was aware now, where I hadn't always been in the past, what a powerful persuader it could be. And how profligately one could employ it.

Although the surviving correspondence was one-sided, it was apparent from my father's letters that the year before he had gone through some profound trauma that had sapped his desire to enter the rabbinate and even his will to live. From the information Dr. Marcus had given me, I figured the crisis had to do with my father's change of heart toward his classmate's sister, to whom he had been engaged. The HUC faculty, largely composed of highly proper Europeans, would have sternly censured my father. "Trifling with a young lady's affections" is the way they might have expressed it.

In any case, even at that tender age my father appears to have cut quite a swathe among the young Jewish female society of Cincinnati, sufficiently wide to set gossip seething. My mother apparently had to take more than a modicum of flak, because rumor was beginning to link her to my father. Her loyalty fuse sputtered and exploded; she was "forced to lose my temper" and tell several of the nosier, bolder tale-bearers to "hold their tongues". And reading that now, with much of the course in view, I reflected on the aptness of the overworked Santayana aphorism, about those who fail to remember the past being doomed to repeat it.

My father wrote: "I ask you no longer to deny that there is anything between us." But they both seemed uneasy about informing my mother's father that they were "engaged." They appeared to dread his indignation, likely because he would also have heard some of the gossip flying around. I thought about the reticent, mild-mannered man I later came to know and love, whose most ferocious act seemed his brisk, determined stride. Perceptions and generations. When my father was 22 and my mother two years younger, the angry whistling of my grandfather's breathing tube could very well have sounded terrifying.

At that age, my father was not yet the soul of tact. At least I first assumed it was insensitivity and a measure of conceit, not a transparent gambit to make my mother jealous that allowed him to write: "Mimi Hochhimer chatted with me for about an hour. She is about twenty-eight, so don't worry, dearest. But I could see that she was fooled like so many into imagining this fat old bum interesting. It is queer how I am able to make some people think that, isn't it?" Then he must have had a twinge, because he added, "And yet, so long as I am able to make you think it—and may that be all my life—I shall be happy. Indeed, under the inspiration of making you think it, I may even be able to make myself really interesting and worthwhile."

Then as I looked over the words again, something else started to come clear. Gaucherie aside, what my father wrote may have had little or nothing to do with conceit. Very possibly he *did* believe he wasn't at all attractive to women. They found him so, but despite the fact that they showed it, he may very well have considered himself an imposter. That wasn't what he wanted to be. So did he then spend all his life conquering with intent to prove?

The resonances, father to son. Him and his flab, me and my gapped teeth.

Well, we are the sum of our parts, aren't we? Parents to children, forebears to descendants. But where does the genetic imperative stop and free will begin? Does it ever?

The sum of our parts. My brother and I both decidedly resembled the Dryer family in looks. And though we saw each other rarely over the years, we had many of the same mannerisms, die-pressed from those of my mother and her brothers. Playing back the tape of the talk Ed and I had in Los Angeles, I found our voices and speech patterns virtually indistinguishable and, again, maternal echoes.

But basically, I am my father's son. Partly, perhaps, through unconscious striving. I'm much shyer than he was, and I couldn't begin to match him as an orator. But I do know from having compared recordings that whenever I spoke from the pulpit, or on radio or TV, my voice magically metamorphosed into a replica of my father's. And in going through his papers, I found passage after passage indicating that as young men, not only our feelings but our thought processes were the same.

Whether as a result of nature or nurture, here I am.

And there I was, gathering evidence about my father and becoming appalled.

A while ago a British filmmaker observed, "We spend our lives repeating our parents' mistakes." To that I have to add: sometimes even when we don't realize our parents have made them.

To an outsider it may have been evident before now. But at last I myself could comprehend why I'd been so exasperatingly stop-start in searching out the details of my father's life.

I had in the past made him out to be a hero. Understandably. It was also predictable that he'd turn out to be less of a white knight than I'd been hoping. But I hadn't anticipated how much less.

At this point I believed that my father's behavior was — to put it baldly — rotten. It hurt me then to think that, and even to write it now is painful. But if he was what he was, and I've inherited some of his less attractive traits, what am I?

I'm alive, that's what.

Thus during the spring days following our Baltimore trip my passion to vindicate my father and my fear that I wouldn't.

* * *

A reply arrived from Jonah. "My memory fails," he wrote, "to recall the slightest friction twixt your wonderful Dad and myself...He called me to be his first assistant. I was delighted to come to the side of this genuine patron of Social Justice in the Reform movement. He was an inspiration to hundreds of us...Philosophically, if memory indeed forgets unpleasantness and beams on the positive, I am a victim. I have not the slightest recollection of friction. My admiration for your father was of heavenly reach. When he departed for those heavens I felt I had lost a father, a teacher, an inspiration."

I sent Jonah a letter of thanks, observing that everyone views the past through his or her peculiar set of prisms, and that he and I obviously differed in our perception of events.

I had almost finished working through the material I'd copied from the Archives. There were just a few more sundry items, mainly to do with my father's social action battles. Such as an attack on his perennial enemy, Maryland's Governor Ritchie, for ostentatiously having done nothing to prevent the lynching of a Negro in Princess Anne County.

There were also some accounts pertaining to the 1933 Scottsboro affair, in which nine Alabama Negro men were sentenced to death by a corrupt court for allegedly raping two white women. A Montgomery rabbi, Benjamin Goldstein, courageously protested the sentence from his pulpit.

The terrified board of his temple immediately fired him. My father, then head of the Social Justice Commission of the Central Conference of American Rabbis, tried to persuade the Conference to put pressure on the Montgomery congregation to rehire its rabbi. Though the Conference had often acted decisively and positively on social questions, they fudged on this one. Too many southern Jews—and their rabbis—lived in perpetual fear of redneck choler.

Then, almost on cue, my father rocked me again. Attempting to cross-reference some minor allusion in my notes, I re-read his letters to my mother. Or thought I was re-reading until I came to one I was sure I'd never seen before. As I read, I wished I weren't seeing it now, My guess is I *had* seen it, and my mind had simply refused to register it.

My father was writing about a regiment of black soldiers bivouacked near an embarcation point in France. The men were getting ready to go home, and they were ecstatic. My father described their uninhibited singing and dancing. Only a couple of paragraphs, but both were splashed with references to "southern niggers," "darkies" and "coons".

Another long, troubled walk. I wasn't entirely surprised by the discovery. My father had spent his youth in the border-southern milieu I myself knew well. When I was growing up, I had my father to help head off my incipient bigotry.

Whatever my father's problematic attitudes when he was 22, there was no trace of them three or four years later. Nor ever again so far as I could ascertain. Throughout his career he had many times, in Dr. Marcus' words, "put his ass on the line" for black causes.

Finally I decided that, tempting as it might be to ignore the references, if I wanted to write honestly about my father, I had to include them. Still, trying to figure how I'd handle it, in conjunction with what I'd learned about his womanizing, was making me uneasy again.

Before I could begin yet another reprise of my yes-no dance, two things happened.

The first involved a couple named Ruth and Marvin Fisher. Once they had been among my parents' most intimate friends. During the crisis in 1939, when Gerald and Naomi and several others began their clamorous denunciation, the Fishers had remained loyal. Ruth was a warm, voluble woman, her husband quieter, gentler, steadfast.

The steadfastness cracked six months later. Suddenly, Ruth and Marvin and my parents were no longer speaking. The Fishers became vehement allies of Gerald and Naomi. I never knew exactly what had happened.

Now I learned that Rachel, the Fishers' daughter, was still living in Baltimore. She was a year or so older than I. Possibly because of that age difference, so important in adolescence, we'd never been close. But we'd certainly been friendly. I took a chance and wrote her, then phoned. Would she agree to talk with me about the rift between our parents? She was at first reluctant, then said she would.

And at just about the same moment I found out that Selma's daughter Marge was living in New Haven.

Ten

Her voice on the phone sounded much as I remembered it — not quite as deep as her mother's, but with the same slightly granular edge. We had a cordial, somewhat breathless conversation. Yes, of course she'd try to help me, with her own memories of my father, and with whatever she knew about the relationship between him and Selma. A lot of her information had come via her sister Elaine, who had died in the late 1970s, but she'd do her best.

We traded capsule interims. Marge's husband was also from Baltimore. They'd met at the end of the War and married ten days later. Julie, a concert violinist and teacher, had also for nearly four decades directed the Starlight Festival, a musical gala held every summer in the courtyards of Yale. Marge had been a psychiatric social worker for the state, then set up a private practice. She and Julie had three children.

I gave her the same sort of cursory fill-in. We were meeting at the end of the month. Details had kept for fifty years; we joked that we might be able to remember them for three more weeks.

I spent much of the time before leaving for New Haven trying to find out what had turned my father's social attitudes around so radically. In 1919 he was at the very least naive, probably reflexively prejudiced, and a little smug about it. But by 1923, when he took over the pulpit in Baltimore, he had become a full-fledged barn-burner — metaphorically — for progressive causes.

There must once have been papers documenting that period: correpondence, sermons, maybe even a diary. I could find nothing now. Nor could I remember his having ever said anything to me that might shed some light on his conversion. A transformation that must have been as weighty for him then as it was mysterious for me now.

Maybe, I thought for a while, his social consciousness had simply evolved. Four years can be a long time when you're in your early twenties. He read a lot, he observed, and from all that perhaps he gradually began to formulate his philosophy. Somehow, though, I couldn't buy that. It didn't sound like my passionate, impulsive father. More likely some person, some event, some personal revelation had led him up to, then thrust him past a critical barrier. But who, what?

I wrote letters, made a spate of phone calls, looking for the answer. Rabbis, the families of my father's political associates, Dr. Marcus. Everyone was intrigued. No one could help.

Then one day, leafing again through the 1930 diary, I came on a passage that had slid past me on first reading, before I'd been exposed to my father's mini-catalogue of patronizing pejoratives.

This was written toward the end of his western swing. The return trip took him into Indiana. He had spent from late 1920 till 1923 as the rabbi in Evansville, and during this time lectured frequently in communities across the state. Passing through Vincennes in 1930 triggered a memory. "The scene of some of my numerous Rotary and Kiwanis and what-not speeches in the days before I became a pink social reformer and was still an exultant Babbit with only a slight rumble of resentment at myself now and then to give any indication of my future revolt. And then, the rumble of resentment would have been silenced, I am sure, did not experience bring to me in a marvelous manner, the sense of real values."

The end. Not a word more. Anywhere. Oh, my papa. Thanks for your help.

My father's first congregation after returning from France was Springfield, Illinois. There he became friendly with the poet Vachel Lindsay, a man of extravagant populist sentiments. I wondered if Lindsay could have been the catalyst. He was 17 years older than my father and had freewheeled around the United States, earning pittances by reciting his poetry, a colorful forerunner of American romantics like Kerouac. Anyone who in those days wrote lines like "Highly establish/ In the name of

God,/ The United States of Europe, Asia and the World" could have lighted a fire under my keen, impressionable but still "Babbitish" father.

It was a seductive possibility. Too seductive, I reluctantly concluded. My father had spoken warmly of the poet, but seldom and always rather casually. There was never even a hint that Lindsay had revolutionized his social values, let alone "in a marvelous manner".

An HUC mate of mine who had been a special admirer of my father suggested that Abraham Cronbach might have been the influence I was looking for. Professor Cronbach had taught at the College, and during the 1920s built an impressive reputation with his writings and speeches on social affairs. Cronbach probably should have been a Quaker, but he would probably have been too emotional for them. He was the most militant pacifist I've ever known. War was a scurvy, Cronbach preached, a pestilence we must eradicate from the face of the earth, swiftly and decisively, but never with even a hint of force. Only through moral suasion. The angrier those who disagreed with you became, the more serene a countenance you should show them. Your example would win them over.

By the time I met Dr. Cronbach in 1939 when I was an HUC freshman, he had become a parody of himself, albeit a courageous one. Crony, as we students called him behind his back, wore a large yellow star armband as a protest against Nazi persecution of the Jews. Not only did he display it at the College and on the streets of Cincinnati; he sought out meetings of the American Nazi Bunds and marched up and down outside the halls, flaunting his badge. His appearance was striking: long, ascetic face, his head completely bald on top but with a bushy crop of white backhair that haloed with every movement. It's doubtful that even those brown-shirted jackals would have attacked him, but it took guts to demonstrate in front of their lairs. And perverseness: if they had assaulted him, Crony would have considered it a personal triumph.

He spoke in a raspy voice, whose singsong was exacerbated by a midwestern twang. Nonetheless, his public exhortations were so fervent — and filled with such genuine social compassion — that he was in demand as a speaker. He was scrupulous in his accounting to the organizations that sponsored his appearances. If a dinner was served, Crony would either not eat, or he would deduct what he estimated the meal cost from the agreed fee. However, he would add on three cents for the stamp he had bought to mail his expense claim.

I knew my father had begun a doctoral dissertation (never completed) under Cronbach. But that was in the late 1920s, when my father's activism had already moved into high gear. And Cronbach didn't begin teaching at the College until 1922, three years after my father graduated. Still, Evansville wasn't that far from Cincinnati. Though there was no evidence to support the conjecture, my father could have fallen under Crony's spell in that period and moved toward greater social consciousness.

Dr. Marcus thought not. "I doubt very much that your dad was influenced by Cronbach," he wrote. "I also suspect that Cronbach was a little too extreme for your father. Ed Israel always had his feet on the ground. He was realistic; Cronbach floated."

And so I had to let that particular puzzle lie. Only for the moment, I hoped.

* * *

The showoff impulses of adolescence may mute with time, but they seldom vanish altogether. I had visions of bounding up onto Marge's porch, clearing steps two or three at a clip. Something like the old farts at the Academy Awards who sprint up the aisle to collect their Oscars, fearful if they don't, all the attendant 13-year-old executive producers will think their blood has stopped circulating.

As it happened, the day before I left for New Haven, my lower back went into its semi-annual freezeup. Oh great, I thought, The Return of Quasimodo the Elder. The pain let up a bit on the drive down, but my passage from the car to Marge's front door still ended up being pretty circumspect. Just as well, because the woman who answered my ring, while as winsome and perky as I recalled her, was also no longer 22.

I was prepared by now for the impact of old relationships abruptly rejoined, but the reunion with Marge was unique. We were pleased that we seemed to communicate easily and immediately, as if there'd been no half-century hiatus. Beneath the cheery surface, however, lay a lot of emotional subtext. So much spoken and unspoken, or spoken and forgotten.

We went out to the kitchen and I helped Marge get food out of the fridge for lunch. Her husband was going to join us momentarily, and I had something I needed to say first. "Back in 1943," I began, "when I just walked away without an explanation..." I knew I wasn't coming at this very gracefully, nor had I expected to. "I didn't understand it then. I wasn't really close to my mother, and anyhow I thought it was my life and yours, not hers. But in the end I guess it did matter. I just couldn't handle it."

"Of course," Marge said quietly. Then she grinned and added with just a touch of sisterly exasperation. "I knew that."

Julie came into the kitchen, a bulky man with a profundo voice, as opinionated as I. Before I left New Haven, we would have a couple of spirited political discussions. We would also talk, at length and less heatedly, about many other things, including the part of stratified Baltimore he came from. Julie's family was Russian-Jewish. He'd grown up in the center of that community, a neighborhood of squat row houses south of Pimlico.

Marge came from old German-Jewish stock on both sides. At the time she met Julie, most German Jews would sooner accept a gentile into the family than a Russian Jew. But Marge was always her own person, and she had no time for parochialism. Because she was beautiful, the crowd we grew up with treated her with a certain deference. They also considered her a maverick. Still did, I informed her now, there was that tone of voice when they told me nobody had heard of her in ages. She laughed. Baltimore was not a place she frequently rushed back to.

Marge and Julie live on a quiet street not far from the Yale campus. The house is old and comfortably laid out, spacious rooms with lots of wood paneling. Julie's practice room, several violins in evidence, branches off one side of a large entrance hall. After lunch, Marge and I settled into leather chairs in the smaller library-office off the other side of the hall.

She had searched out a number of photographs. Her parents, together and separately. Selma, assured and soignee in every shot, looking — as the saying used to go — like she'd stepped out of a bandbox. Marge in her teens, Elaine, one of my father leaning over some papers on his desk, cigarette in hand, rumpled and intent.

I studied the snaps of Walter, Marge's father. I hadn't known him well. It was Selma I saw most when I was at their house. But even if Walter had been around more, I doubt we'd have got to be friends. Leaving aside my shyness and who I was, I always found Walter cold, almost forbidding. He was fair, balding, with fine features and very light, unwavering eyes. He wore elegantly designed glasses, sometimes rimless, sometimes delicately edged with gold. I remember him as being bright and well-informed, probably an intellectual snob.

Marge half-confirmed this now. "When your parents first got to Baltimore," she told me, "they and my parents were a foursome. For a while they went everywhere together. But my father didn't like your mother, and the foursome came apart pretty quickly."

I could see my mother, still pretty then, but unstylishly dressed, poorly read, neither vital nor witty. But not insensitive. Probably feeling wretched every time Walter's pale, contemptuous eyes flicked past her as if she didn't exist.

What had my father thought? Had all those flaming declarations of love, so recently uttered, begun to dissipate now? Or had they already faded?

"That was in 1923," I said, thinking aloud. "Which meant it was quite a while after that before your mother and my father got together."

Marge raised her eyebrows. "Not according to Elaine. Unless you consider a few months quite a while."

I needed some moments to assimilate that one. I thought about Roberta Gordon and the other women I'd heard about. I told Marge what I knew.

She had always been difficult to surprise. Even when we were kids, it was if she was already the therapist who'd seen and heard everything.

She started to talk about Selma, almost, I realized, by way of explanation. Her mother, Marge said, had a powerful intellectual curiosity and enormous social drive. She was a terrific volunteer, a bundle of energy. And of contradictions.

She could be charming and flamboyantly generous. Sometimes she was a warm and attentive mother, but there was also a single-minded, selfish streak. "She spent more of her time," Marge observed drily, "on Child Study than on her children."

Apparently, Selma loved sex, and needed it. She cared deeply for my father and had the temerity to carry on the long affair with him. Yet it was important to her what people thought. Beneath her veneer of savoir-faire, she was really very dependent. When Walter died suddenly in Maine and I drove my father across the state to be with her, she was fine as long as he was there. But the next day, she began to contemplate her future as a widow. Especially her social life. "I'll be a third wheel," she lamented to Marge, meaning that in those days no one invited an extra woman of a certain age to smart dinner parties.

This didn't seem to jibe with the impression I'd been carrying around. That summer of 1941, my father was preparing to take over his Union job. After Walter's death he and Selma probably began making plans for the future. Certainly by the time my father died—judging from Selma's letter that I found in his room—there was an understanding. After a relatively few, albeit messy, months, she and my father could finally have been together. Why then—ignoring for the moment the tinge of callousness—Selma's concern about being alone?

Maybe they had decided it would be wiser to avoid doing anything consequential for a while. True, my father's new position would be perceived as much more secular, removed from the moral expectations of a congregation. And divorce for rabbis was by then deemed thinkable, if not yet *comme il faut*. Still, some of my father's Union Executive Board consisted of highly proper, old line rabbis, and a number of the lay members thought as well as spoke like nineteenth century burghers. My father hardly needed a damaging scandal as his inaugural gesture.

He would have spent much of his initial year in office on the road, building a grass roots following, cementing leadership alliances. I knew his plans at the time included only occasional visits to Baltimore. Selma would have been free to travel, but if indeed their decision was to cool things temporarily, their meetings would have been sporadic and still somewhat clandestine.

I thought again about my mother's stricken expression as she watched my father and me leave our Maine cottage to go comfort his lover, the new widow. His total lack of expression. The cruelty and selfishness, or the threshold of fulfillment, depending on the beholder. I know whose side I was on then. Sitting in Marge's library, I was no longer so sure I'd been right.

"What about your father?" I asked her. "He must have known." Marge nodded. "Didn't he care, or what?"

"He cared," Marge said. "According to Elaine—Mother never spoke to me about it—one problem was they were sexually incompatible. I always thought they were incompatible in other ways, too. He hated the 'social whirl' she found so important, and he was always putting down her closest women friends, they weren't intellectual enough for him."

One area where they did connect, though, was bridge. Both Walter and Selma played savage games. So, I recalled now, did my father, while my mother was more inclined to float comfortably through her sessions at the table.

"My father was in New York a lot on business," Marge went on. "Elaine thought he had someone there, a buyer. I can't be sure, but my feeling is that never amounted to anything. What I do think was important, I can't ever remember him mentioning your father, not once. And while my mother went to temple every single week and sat in the pew hanging on every word your father said, or just looking at him, my father was very vehement about *not* going, ever. So I think he felt it all right, yeah, he cared."

She didn't say anything for a moment, then shook her head. "The thing I've always wondered about with our parents—where did they get together? I mean, they couldn't just run off to a hotel, not in Baltimore."

A memory, very nebulous, began stirring, possibly evoked by Marge's telling me when she believed the affair had actually started. Sitting in a parked car on Eutaw Place, aged — what, seven, eight? — reading, waiting. Glancing up. Rows of huge trees, symmetrically planted on either side of the street, leafy branches overreaching to form a sun-dappled canopy. Reading, glancing up again. The front door of one of the houses across the street opening, Selma emerging, hurrying down the white stone steps, getting into her car and driving away. For a few moments then, nothing, only the grey stone housefront, one of a rank. A passerby, moving languidly in the summer afternoon heat. Then my father.

"Manny," I said. "They met at Manny's." Dr. Manfried, as he was more properly known. My father's and Selma's physician, my father's close friend. One of the many doctors along Eutaw Place who lived above their ground-floor offices.

"Not at Manny's," Marge said. "I can't believe it." But as the memory grew, and with it an intimation of its not having been an isolate, I could. And after a while so could she. Manny as Friar Laurence.

It struck us then how bizarre it was to be sitting here discussing what furtive moves our parents might have made all those years before.

"She really was extraordinary," Marge mused. "I can understand how men would fall in love with her. But she could be willful, too. Even cruel."

Selma married twice after Walter and my father died, hastily and to a mismatched partner each time. She scheduled the second of these weddings for the exact hour when Marge would be graduating from the Pennsylvania School of Social Work. "She knew the date of those graduation ceremonies as well as I. Whether it was just thoughtless or unconsciously competitive, I don't know. But she wouldn't change her plans, and it hurt a lot."

Capricious and egotistical though she may have been, her daughters adored her. In her seventies, lying in intensive care after a pair of massive heart attacks, she looked up at Marge and Elaine with an insouciant grin and called out, "It's been a great life with you girls." Very soon afterward she died. Marge's eyes filled with tears as she remembered.

Marge had loved my father, and though she had been aware of his impatient nature, she hadn't understood how truly difficult he could sometimes be. Just as I hadn't known what Selma was really like. We talked for a while about being the children of powerful, mercurial parents, how their influence alternately inspired and battered us.

I wondered what my father and Selma might have been like as a couple.

Always, all those years, they were shimmering on each other's horizons. If they had ever got together, it might have ended up as mutual assured destruction. On the other hand, both of them were brilliant, attractive and ambitious. Selma would have understood his activist goals and could have been an astute co-strategist. Together in social circles, they would have sparkled. Had my father survived his clogged arteries, Selma's and his excitement over a parade of triumphs may have served as a perennial aphrodisiac. And, perhaps, shunted off domestic discord.

Selma remained devastated for a long time after my father died. She believed, however, in life after death, and was certain that sooner or later she would be reunited with him. During the first few months following my father's death, Selma's phone would ring almost every day, at exactly the minute when he used to call her. There was never anyone on the line. But she was convinced the calls were my father's efforts to talk to her from the nether world. Marge, watching her mother's face as she rushed to answer the phone, listening to her voice, became even more aware of how much Selma cared for my father.

Shortly before I left New Haven, Marge dropped a bombshell. Her father, she remembered, sometime around 1935 — maybe the year after, but no later — had written a letter to the Har Sinai board. He was writing for the record, Walter stated flatly. All rumors concerning his wife and Rabbi Israel were categorically untrue.

Marge felt Walter wrote the letter primarily to protect Selma — and probably himself — from scandal. But in 1935 or '36? That would mean gossip was circulating several years before the crisis I knew about. Rumors sufficiently serious to provoke Walter into denying them.

Why hadn't the congregation fired my father then?

It gave me something else to puzzle over on the road to Baltimore.

ELEVEN

Although it was nearly midnight when I dropped Rachel Fisher Steinberg off at the entrance to her apartment building, the temperature was still close to 80 degrees, the air supersaturated. Typical Baltimore summer weather, and had been all day. Blast-furnace heat juiced up by a succession of torrential thunderstorms.

I drove north up deserted Park Heights Avenue, in the opposite direction from my hotel. It probably wasn't a good idea to go where I was heading, but I wanted to do it.

It had been a long, emotional day. A lot of it was enjoyable. Rachel was good company — upbeat, a proud grandmother but funny about it, nearly as wryly loquacious as her own mother but not as bristly.

Despite our being glad to see each other, we sparred warily for a few minutes. The rancor between our families had been devastating, and even this long afterward Rachel wasn't sure she wanted to talk about what she termed "a lot of really rough stuff". But then we started reminiscing about the good times. For both Rachel and me, the memories were a return to innocence. Improvised picnic suppers in the back yard of one family or the other. Everybody dressed sloppily and maybe drinking a little too much, as people tended to in those days, but at total ease with one another. My father doing impersonations of public figures, cracking up all the Fishers and himself. My mother rosy and happy.

Rachel's parents weren't intellectuals. They knew my father knew they weren't, and that in other compartments of his life he would relate to other people on completely different levels. They also knew there was nothing condescending in his enjoyment of being with them. They were crazy about him. As was Rachel. "I worshipped that man," she said. "Absolutely worshipped him."

We spent the afternoon together, sitting in her air-conditioned apartment, while the sky outside alternately glittered and darkened. In the evening we drove across town to Bo Brooks, a restaurant for serious devotees of the Chesapeake Bay crab. You sit at rough wooden tables thickly carpeted with newspaper and order crabs by the dozen, large if they're available, all sizes torridly seasoned. The server dumps them onto the newspaper and hands each person a wooden mallet. You crack the shells, probe for the sweet, spicy morsels of meat and wash them down with beer.

Rachel and I shouted at each other over the din of mallets and nasal C & W from the jukebox. Off and on we continued to reminisce, as we had all afternoon. Interspersed with nostalgia came the "rough stuff".

"I have to tell you right away," Rachel said when we finally jumped into the nitty-gritty, "I'm a friend of Jonah. I was back then, and I am today. Your father—you know how I always felt about him, and I still do. But..." There were tears in her eyes. "He was such a jerk."

Jonah, according to Rachel, had caught my father in his study *en flagrante* with Selma. Or almost. When Jonah walked into the room, Selma was lying on the couch and my father was zipping up his fly.

If that's what really took place, I thought, in his study in the temple, Rachel's right, he *was* a jerk. I also thought: what ever happened to the quaint custom of knocking on doors? But I kept quiet. Confrontation wasn't my reason for being there.

Jonah was shocked of course, Rachel continued, but he hadn't blown the whistle. No, I thought, maybe not directly. But he obviously mentioned what he'd seen, or how would Rachel have known? If indeed he had seen it.

"I wrote Jonah," I said. "He wrote back that he couldn't remember a single minute of bad feeling between himself and my father."

"Why should he tell you anything?" Rachel demanded.

"I can think of lots of reasons why he might not want to," I replied. And that, fortunately, was as close as we came to collision all day.

However, her question was relevant enough. Why *should* Jonah tell me anything, and possibly revive an interlude that for one reason or another he'd just as soon forget? Or maybe, as he implied, he really had forgotten it, and preferred to keep the lid tamped firmly against any possibility of recall.

I asked Rachel if her parents had known about my father and Selma before Jonah's discovery. Rachel said they'd suspected, and even heard rumors, but they hadn't been sure. Even after their suspicions were confirmed, they didn't do anything about it.

"Why not?" I asked.

"They loved your father," she replied simply. "They felt awful about it, but he was their friend."

The blowoff came, according to Rachel, when my mother discovered (how wasn't clear) that Ruth and Marvin knew. She was livid with them for not having said anything to her, and the years-long intimacy ended abruptly.

Soon after the break, Rachel recalled, things hotted up rapidly at Har Sinai. She was fuzzy about details, but she thought that in the spring of 1941 the board asked my father to resign. And luckily for him, just at that point the offer arrived from the Union.

Later, I checked the board minutes for that year. There were no indications, overt or implied, of the kind of tension Rachel was describing. However, working with the UN had made me all too familiar with official euphemism.

There were numerous discrepancies—time and circumstance—in the version of events Rachel was giving me. It didn't matter. She was telling me what she remembered, as objectively as she could. It was generous of her to do it, and I had re-established a warm tie with the past.

What she'd told me *was* rough stuff. But for what I was trying to do, I needed to have heard it. On the way back from Bo Brooks, I asked Rachel, "As long as we're talking so frankly, tell me, do you ever remember hearing anything about my father and other women besides Selma?"

She looked surprised, then shook her head. "If there had been, I'm sure I'd have heard. I never did."

She sounded very positive. I grabbed hold of what she told me without thinking, immensely relieved.

* * *

I parked in front of the house, turned off the headlights and sat in the darkness, hoping no one would spot me and think I was casing the place for a B and E.

Off to the right, beyond the hedge, at the border of what had once been a vacant lot, that was where the goat had been tethered. My father had brought it home one evening, sitting beside him in the front seat of the car, God knows how he'd got it to stay quiet during the drive. Or when he honked the horn to call us out of the house. But we all came running—my mother, my brother and I.

My mother looked at my father. She knew the last thing we needed was a goat, and so did he. In a couple of months it would end up on a farm. But that was later. This was now. My father had seen the goat in a pet shop, he said. It had taken to him.

"Well," my mother said slowly, continuing to look at my father, "I guess we should tie him up over there, shouldn't we?"

"Her," my father said. My mother smiled. So did my father. He put his arm around her. "Thanks," he said.

If only she hadn't tried to be different, if only she hadn't let him railroad her into trying to change. Maybe eventually he'd have come to accept her for what she was—her warmth, her slow sweetness, her dedicated loyalty—and to prize it.

No, I thought then, I've been saying that, but I'm wrong, I've been wrong the whole time. Yes, he might have come to value highly what she was. I think in a way he already did. But it still wouldn't have worked. He needed the sharpness, the complexity, the challenge to his imagination that Selma must have provided, and my mother never could.

I remembered a summer day in my grandmother's Cincinnati hotel when I was six or seven. My father and I were coming down the front steps just as a Boston bull pup wandered onto the lawn. The dog saw my father, made a beeline for him and pressed himself against his leg, shivering. He was obviously lost and terrified, no license or even a collar. My father picked him up and stroked him. After a few minutes the puppy stopped shaking and licked my father's face.

My father put an ad in the paper. For three days no one responded, and my father and the puppy were already treating each other like lifelong friends. The morning of the fourth day a man phoned, described the dog well enough to convince my father, and came to pick him up. My father watched despondently as the man and the puppy drove away.

A couple of hours later, I knocked on the open door of my parents' bedroom, then stopped in the doorway, distressed. I wanted to run away, but I couldn't. In any case, no one was paying the slightest attention to me. My father was lying face down on the bed, sobbing, an awful wracking sound that went on and on. My mother was sitting very still in a chair a few feet away, her expression anguished.

I didn't understand why my father was crying, but even at that age I sensed somehow it didn't really have anything to do with the loss of the dog.

The summer I was fifteen, my father was scheduled to give a series of lectures at the University of Virginia. He asked if I wanted to come with him for a few days of deep-sea fishing before he went to Charlottesville. His friend Frank Graham at the University of North Carolina had recommended Ocracoke, one of the islands forming the Hatteras barrier.

We left the car in a tiny mainland fishing village and rode the ferry, a rusting barge powered by an erratic two-cylinder diesel, out to Ocracoke. The map showed the island to be about ten miles long and maybe half a mile wide. What we could see from the ferry was mostly sand and scrub grass, some stunted trees and a few bare-board houses. In those days hardly anyone went there, and few of the inhabitants ever came to the mainland. A couple of families dominated the island, and they'd been intermarrying for generations.

We checked into the hotel, a weathered frame shack with half a dozen Spartan rooms. When we came down to dinner, a few men were sitting around the lobby, which also served as a dining room. The windows were open, and there was a strong smell of the sea, overlaid with something faintly but pervasively musty. Everyone was very polite, and a little distant. They spoke in a strange, stilted style that wasn't quite archaic but sounded as if it should be.

They watched us in silence as we tucked into gigantic bowls of fish chowder. When we'd emptied them, my father got up and carried the empty bowls over to the proprietor, who had a gleaming hairless skull and beefy, tattooed forearms. "Finished?" he asked.

"More," my father said, and suddenly everyone began talking again, not directly to us, but it felt as if we were included. "Be a full moon tonight," the proprietor said as he plunked down our chowder refills. "You might ought to look for the horses."

In 1732, he explained, an Arabian ship bound for Virginia with a cargo of prize breeding stock, foundered in one of the treacherous Hatteras storms. The horses now running wild on Ocracoke were descendants of a few that had managed to swim ashore from the wreck.

We trudged across the island toward the ocean side. The sky was cloudless, and moonlight gave the sand an eerie, bleached luster. Gradually the sound of surf grew louder. Then there was something else. My father heard it first and stopped walking.

They came into sight galloping flat out, maybe two dozen of them, manes flying, led by a magnificent stallion. I couldn't tell his real color, but under the moon he looked brilliant copper all over, almost like red ocher. They passed so close I could hear their snorting and ragged breathing over the muffled thunder of their hooves. Then they were gone, vanished as if they'd been a mirage, and there was only the distant beating of the surf.

I heard my father let out his breath, a long sigh, and I realized I'd also been holding mine. He sighed again, took out a pack of cigarettes, then returned it to his pocket. "I went to Manny last week for a checkup," he said, and added when he glanced at my face, "It's okay, he said I'm fine. As fine as somebody with the kind of heart I have can be. I..." He stopped. After a few seconds he put his hand on my shoulder. I looked at him. I think I must have been holding my breath again. "Manny said if I retire, if I turn my back on the crazy kind of life I lead, just stop, well then, I'll have a very good chance of getting old."

He took his hand off my shoulder and said, "I haven't talked to your mother about this, she..." He stopped again and shook his head. "I've thought about it. I can't tell you how appealing the idea is. A little place in Florida, not Miami, somewhere over on the Gulf coast, Key West, or maybe even California. Fishing, reading, writing, maybe a speech now and then to help pay the bills. The peace..." He grimaced. "I just can't do it, you know, son. No. That's a lie. I don't want to do it. I'm cut out for what I do. If I try to turn my back on that, I—What I'm trying to say is I've thought about it, hard, and I've made my choice. I don't mean to frighten or upset you, but I wanted you to know how I feel."

He looked at me, I guess to see if I understood. I couldn't say anything, but I guess he knew I did. His hand was on my shoulder again, and both of us turned to see if maybe the horses would come back.

TWELVE

After I returned from my second trip to Baltimore, I let some time go by before trying to write about it, because I wanted to get it all into proper perspective. Now, glancing over what I set down, I see that I haven't, really.

Mainly, because I wanted so much for it to be true, I believed Rachel's conviction that there were no other women in my father's married life except my mother and Selma. I don't especially believe it now, though I would still like to. But all that smoke blowing from all those directions, ignore it and sooner or later the fire will sneak up and burn you.

Maybe over the length of the relationship with Selma — nearly two decades, longer than many marriages today — there were frustrations that set him desperate. Maybe — and I see that even now I'm trying to rationalize, provide him with excuses. I have to understand that there can be an infinity of reasons, but none that add up to an excuse. Accept this, and I can begin to accept my father. And — dare I say it — maybe myself? It isn't easy, but at no point in our life together did he ever promise me easy.

A while back, checking once again through the accumulation of research material, I came across an article my father wrote in November, 1932, just a few weeks before his experience in Washington with the Hunger Marchers. "The only truly dynamic revolutionary must be religious," part of it ran. "It is the only thing that can give harmony and sequence to his philosophy of life. It is the only thing that can keep him eternally a revolutionary. It is the only thing that can give meaning to his striving for humanity. Faith in a cosmic unity is the only safeguard against dictatorial arrogance on the one hand and cynical despair on the other.

"Today we advocate pacifism, the abolition of the profit system and the more practical realization of democracy. We advocate these salient points because humanity is cursed specifically by war, by economic exploitation and by a throttling of the freedom of the individual in political and civil expression. Tomorrow it may be an entirely different set of social evils which will distort humankind. Radical religion will change its set of concrete goals. Its guiding principle of a striving for full human expression will remain. The static revolutionary might be satisfied with the realization of a pacifistic, socialistic society. His end has been achieved. Radical religion is never satisfied. It puts eternal unrest into the hearts of men."

Not a bad credo, I thought, filling up with pride. And I realized too how much the restless energy of his beliefs also drove him personally.

I regret that I haven't yet been able to chart my father's transition from unconscious racist to tough, streetwise battler for equality. It troubled me to mention his early prejudices, but it would have troubled me more to conceal them. What distresses me most is that in the increasingly righteous and inflexible correctness of today's world, some who read this might denounce the beginnings and disregard the progress.

I believe—though I'm still very tentative about it—that I may finally have some insight into the problem that's been baffling me almost since the first moment I decided to write about my father.

Many if not most of his congregation knew what a shambles his personal life was. Especially during his last years in Baltimore there was a faction that tried repeatedly to get rid of him. Each time, a staunch group of defenders thwarted their efforts.

It's possible, as my brother and some others have suggested, that my father had become so well known, so much of an icon, that even his enemies felt ambivalent about toppling him. But more famous personalities than my father have been brought down, for less blatant transgressions—some even in latter days, at the height of the sexual revolution.

Also, by the end of his tenure in Baltimore, my father was more famous and powerful than he had ever been. Yet this was when the attacks became most vigorous, and very nearly succeeded.

But again and again, those who tried to oust him were rebuffed, by the same loyal cadre. And I'm not talking about some oddball fringe. His defenders were prominent doctors, lawyers, executives, men and women with impeccable community credentials. I'm certain they all regarded themselves as moral persons. Even Mildred, who Virginia believes was probably in love with my father, was a hardheaded woman, not given to sentimentality in her organizational career. Besides, if she really was besotted with my father, the fact that he was involved with other women wouldn't necessarily make her race to his defense. As she did. As did so many others.

I've come to believe they were not blind to my father's faults. Nor in all likelihood were they very happy about them. I doubt many people enjoy regarding their spiritual leader as flawed, particularly when his frailties have to do with the flesh.

But I think they also recognized over the years my father's unfeigned love and concern for each of them as individuals. His ability to listen to their problems, to provide advice and if necessary active help, might have for them outweighed many of his shortcomings. It's even possible that because they were aware of his failings, they felt he might better understand theirs.

What seems important in the end is not that my father displayed weaknesses. Nor that some in his congregation—with justification—attacked him for his imperfections. Nor that others might have, but refrained because of the national prestige he had earned by his considerable achievements.

What I think it comes down to is that those who fought for him so passionately did so because he was dear to them as a loving, caring human being. They were willing to accept and even cherish him, *despite* his frailties.

If that's true—especially considering the times—they were a remarkable group of men and women, with a greater capacity for understanding, compassion and love than I would have thought possible.

About an hour ago, I looked once more at the minutes of the Union Executive Board meeting at which my father died. This time there were no tears, but I don't think I'll read them again.

I was suddenly aware, though, how much had changed for me between my first encounter with those minutes in the Archives and now.

How long it took me to appreciate the chemistry of my father's combined strengths and weaknesses.

How long it took me to realize that I probably loved him even more than I knew, and that his early death traumatized me more than I thought.

And that now at last I'm at peace with both my love and his death.

THE END

ACKNOWLEDGMENTS

I owe an enormous debt to the late Dr. Jacob R. Marcus, and to the American Jewish Archives in Cincinnati, Ohio, which he founded and directed. Special thanks to Archivist Kevin Proffitt, who assisted greatly with my efforts to bridge gaps in my father's story. The Library Services of *The Baltimore Sun* provided me with additional meaningful research material.

My aunt, Frances Murr Israel, supplied me with an abundance of family anecdotes, to which she added her own distinctive mix of warmth and sharpness.

Old friends were graciously forthcoming: Rabbi Randall M. Falk, Leah Adler, Margery Scheir and her husband Julius.

I'm grateful to Janis Orenstein, Marina Savona and Joni Boyer for having read and commented on the manuscript in its early stages, and to Arlene Lampert for her perceptive editorial suggestions.

A number of Baltimoreans generously spent time with me, reminiscing about my father and the effect he had on their lives. Virginia Gordon was particularly helpful. Herman Kerngood, Martin Dannenberg, Morton Oppenheimer, Phyllis Coplan, Dr. Louis Kaplan and the late Rabbi Abraham Shusterman all provided unique and revealing facets. The late Rabbi Eugene Lipman of Washington, D.C. helped me try to solve the mystery of how my father metamorphosed so dramatically from mild reactionary to warrior for social justice.

While all the events I've described in this book are as accurate as I could make them, I've deliberately changed the names of some of the participants.